MUDDLE EARTH TOO

PESTICIDE THE FLOWER FAIRY

Paul Stewart & Chris Riddell

First published in Great Britain in 2011
by Macmillan Children's Books
This Large Print edition published 2012
by AudioGO Ltd
by arrangement with
Macmillan Publishers Limited

ISBN: 978 1445 842257

British Library Cataloguing in Publication Data available

Printed and bound in Great Britain by
MPG Books Group Limited

For Julie
PS

For Jo
CR

NAME: Joe Jefferson

OCCUPATION: Schoolboy

HOBBIES: Football, TV, arguing with his sister

FAVOURITE FOOD: Anything not cooked by Norbert

NAME: Randalf the Wise, Muddle Earth's . . . er, leading wizard?

OCCUPATION: Wizard Headmaster of Stinkyhogs School of Wizardry

HOBBIES: Performing spells (I think you'll find that's spell! – Veronica)

FAVOURITE FOOD: Norbert's squashed tadpole fritters

NAME: Ella Jefferson

OCCUPATION: Moody big sister to her brother, Joe – and a barbarian princess

HOBBIES: See 'Occupation', plus painting her nails black

FAVOURITE FOOD: Cheeseburger and fries

NAME: Norbert the
Not-Very-Big
OCCUPATION: School cook
HOBBIES: Thumb-sucking,
cooking – especially
cake-decorating
FAVOURITE FOOD:
Everything

NAME: Veronica
OCCUPATION: Familiar to the
great wizard, Randalf the Wise
HOBBIES: Being sarcastic
FAVOURITE FOOD:
Anything not cooked by Norbert

NAME: Walter, once The
Horned Baron, now retired
OCCUPATION: Retired Ruler
of Muddle Earth
HOBBIES: Wooing Fifi the Fair
in their love nest in Trollbridge
FAVOURITE FOOD: Bad-
breath porridge

NAME: Lord Asbow
OCCUPATION: Dean of
University of Whatever
HOBBIES: Repelling invaders,
discussing the meaning of life
with his pet Labrador
FAVOURITE FOOD: Sunrise dust,
dog food

NAME: Edward Gorgeous

OCCUPATION: Student and barbarian

HOBBIES: Broomball, brooding, looking gorgeous

FAVOURITE FOOD: Tomatoes (sort of)

NAME: Edwina Lovely

OCCUPATION: Queen Susan's lady-in-waiting (sometimes)

HOBBIES: Looking lovely, obsessing over Edward Gorgeous

FAVOURITE FOOD: Royal blood

NAME: Eraguff the Eager-to-Please

OCCUPATION: Dragon

HOBBIES: Nest decorating, flower picking, knitting

FAVOURITE FOOD: Definitely NOT wizard

NAME: Eudora Pinkwhistle, one of Muddle Earth's leading witches

OCCUPATION: Potions teacher, Stinkyhogs

HOBBIES: Spells, and crushing on a certain wizard headmaster

FAVOURITE FOOD: Tea and fairy-cake

NAME: Mr Fluffy

OCCUPATION: Woodwork teacher, Stinkyhogs

HOBBIES: Storing food in his chubby cheeks, howling at Muddle Earth's three moons

FAVOURITE FOOD: Nuts

NAME: Kings Peter and Edmund and Queens Susan and Lucy

OCCUPATION: Er . . . Kings and Queens

HOBBIES: Bossing people about

FAVOURITE FOOD: As long as it's expensive, anything!

NAME: Pesticide and Nettle, Thistle and Briar Rose

OCCUPATION: Flower fairies

HOBBIES: Jeer-leading, causing trouble

FAVOURITE FOOD: Pollen pizza

BOOK THREE

Pesticide the Flower Fairy

PROLOGUE

Deep, deep under the ground, in the vast vaulted fairy caverns beneath Harmless Hill, it was breakfast time. At one end of the forty-foot table sat Queen Titania, on her throne of living willow wood with its luxuriant garlands of fragrant flowers. At the other end sat King Oberon, on his leatherette reclining chair with its built-in footrest.

'Pass the acacia honey, Ron,' said his queen in a voice as soft and melodious as dewdrops dripping from dandelions.

'What's that, Tania, my love?' said

3

King Oberon, without looking up from the sports section of the *Fairy Times*.

'The honey, Ron,' Queen Titania said in a voice as light and gentle as a summer breeze in a flower meadow.

'The what?' muttered King Oberon, his gaze fixed on the fairy-football results.

'The acacia honey!' Queen Titania shouted in a voice capable of stunning a stiltmouse at a hundred yards. 'I want it! NOW!'

From high up in the vaulted ceiling came the fluttering of wings as four prim-faced elderly fairies swooped down on to the table. Pushing and jostling one another in their eagerness to please, they seized the silver honey pot at King Oberon's elbow and flew with it to Queen Titania's side. Cooing and clucking, they set the honey pot down and began fussing over the buttercup croissant on their queen's silver plate.

'A spoonful of honey dripped over it? . . .'

'Or shall we cut it in two and spread the honey inside? . . .'

4

'Or cut it into tiny pieces so you can dip it in the honey yourself? . . .'

'Or we can do it for you . . .'

'Thank you, Peaseblossom. Thank you, Cobweb. Thank you, Moth, and you, Mustardseed. That'll be all . . .' She waved them away. 'Put the spoon down, Peaseblossom. Leave the croissant alone, Cobweb. I said, *leave* it, Moth. *And* you, Mustardseed. Drop the

5

butter-knife . . .' The queen's voice rose in irritation as the fairies continued to fuss and flutter around her. 'I said, *that will be all*! Now, shoo! Shoo, the lot of you!'

With prim little exclamations and tiny tutting sounds, Peaseblossom, Cobweb, Moth and Mustardseed flew back to their velvet cushions high up in the vaulted ceiling. Queen Titania sat back exhaustedly in her willow throne and sighed.

'Ron,' she said. 'Put the newspaper down. We need to talk.' She folded her arms. '*Ron!*'

At the other end of the table, King Oberon lowered the *Fairy Times* and scratched the hairy belly that protruded from his stained vest.

'Yes, dear,' he said obediently. 'What about?'

'Our daughter,' said Queen Titania.

'What's she done now?' he said wearily.

'That's just it, Ron,' said the queen. 'She hasn't *done* anything. That school she insisted we send her to—now she says she doesn't need to go back. And as for that camping trip of hers, it turns out she didn't have permission to borrow that chariot after all. I had to deal with a very angry barbarian who kept going on about his missing horned helmet and bearskin coat. And since she got back, all she ever seems to do is mope about in her room with those dreadful friends of hers. And have you seen the state of her room? I looked in the other day, quite innocently, and she got absolutely furious with me. Took her mittens off and waved those awful fingers at me. I'm telling you, Ron, it sent shivers down my spine. Oh, when I think back to her christening . . .'

'Now, don't go upsetting yourself, Tania, my love,' said King Oberon. 'Fairy-tale christenings *can* go wrong. It was just one of those things. Look on the bright side. She could have grown up blue-eyed and beautiful, only to prick her

finger on a spindle and fall asleep for a hundred years.'

'Yes, but Pesticide is such an unfortunate name,' said Queen Titania.

'That's the trouble with wicked fairy godmothers, my love,' said King Oberon, shaking his head. 'But as curses go, Pesticide could have done far worse. So long as she remembers to keep her mittens on, she'll be fine.'

'But she's *not* fine, Ron,' Queen Titania protested. 'You and I both know it. She's . . . Oh, hello, darling,' she gushed, blushing as crimson as a field poppy when she spotted her daughter standing in the doorway of the immense cavern. 'I didn't see you there. Daddy and I were just talking about you, weren't we, Ron?'

Pesticide shrugged and stared at her parents from beneath her fringe of acid-green hair. Her black eyeliner matched her black

8

blouse edged in black spiderweb lace, which went perfectly with her black tutu with its carefully ripped black trim, her neatly laddered black tights and her extra clompy, blacker-than-black boots.

'I'm going out,' she said.

'Out, dear?' said Queen Titania, her voice as lilting as a lark in a lilac tree. 'Out where?'

'Just out,' Pesticide mumbled as she inspected a stray thread at the cuff of one of her black mittens. She looked up. 'Dad,' she said. 'How many aints are there in Elfwood? I goggled it on the inter-elf but I'm still waiting for an answer.'

'Aints?' said King Oberon. 'What on earth are you asking about aints for? That's old old fairy magic, that is. Best left well alone. You'll be asking me about the Trowel of Turbulence next.'

'Oh no, the inter-elf told me all about the trowel *and* the plant pot *and* the . . .' She clamped a mittened hand to her mouth to stop herself. 'Doesn't matter.' She turned on her heels and stomped sulkily off.

'Oh, Ron!' Queen Titania wailed. 'What *are* we going to do with her?'

From the four corners of the cream-coloured castle, ivory white turrets sprouted. Dozens of them. Some were short and squat, others tall and elegant. Some were square, some were round, while some were twisted, like sticks of white barley sugar. All were topped by pointy spires of pale alabaster from which faded calico pennants fluttered.

Set high up in the crenellated walls of the castle were small shuttered windows and cross-shaped arrow-slits, while at its base was a broad arched doorway. Above it, chiselled into the white marble, were the words *University of Whatever*.

The drawbridge to the castle was down and resting on the dusty ground.

'The lamp-post!' Joe called back over his shoulder as he ran on to the drawbridge. 'It went this way!'

Behind him, by some considerable distance, came Norbert, galumphing over the meadow grass. Randalf bounced about on his shoulders, struggling to hold on to his hat. Above them both flew Veronica, her small blue wings a blur of rapid movement.

Further back still strolled Edward and Ella, hand in hand and gazing into one another's eyes.

'Wait, Joe! We don't have time for this!' shouted Randalf. 'We've got to find the Goblet of Porridge, remember?' He waved at him agitatedly.

'Stop! Stop! You have to ring the castle's bell first, or it'll think you're an invader!'

12

Joe paused on the drawbridge and turned. 'What bell? Who'll think I'm an invader? ... *Whoooah!*'

There was a resounding creak and a clatter of chains, and Joe disappeared from view as the drawbridge slammed shut.

'Joe! Joe!' squawked Veronica, flapping towards the castle and disappearing through one of the narrow arrow-slits. Just then, a klaxon sounded.

'That's torn it,' said Randalf as Norbert came to an abrupt halt in front of the castle gate.

On the wall beside the raised drawbridge was a silver doorbell. Beneath it, in small, spiky, difficult-to-read writing, were the words *Castle Admittance Device*, followed by a list of instructions in writing that was even smaller and harder to read.

(a) Raise hand and extend forefinger.

(b) Place said forefinger on circular button marked 'press'.

(c) Apply pressure with aforementioned digit.

(d) Retract said aforementioned digit and await response.

WARNING : INVADERS WILL BE REPELLED!

Edward and Ella approached.

'This place brings back memories,' said Edward with a shudder as he stopped next to Norbert and Randalf, and looked up.

Beside him, Ella gave a puzzled frown. 'Where's Joe?'

Randalf looked down at her from Norbert's shoulder. 'I'm afraid . . .' he began as, from inside the walls, there came the sounds of clanking cogs and grinding gear-wheels. 'Joe has invaded the castle.'

Just then, from high above their heads, there was a loud *WHUMPH!* and a plump vacuum-cleaner bag came sailing over the crenellated walls. It landed at their feet and burst open, sending a cloud of dust billowing into

14

the air and coating the four of them from head to foot. From beneath Randalf's arm the rolled-up stair-carpet gave a choked little gasp.

'Oh! Dust! My worst nightmare . . . Sleepy. *So* sleepy . . . *Zzzzzzzzzz.*'

One by one, Norbert, Randalf, Ella and finally Edward slumped to the ground. There was a second *whumph* and a duvet and four pillows came fluttering gently down. The pillows slipped beneath the sleepers' heads while the duvet settled over their sleeping bodies. Stitched into the duvet cover and pillowcases in small hard-to-read letters were the words *Defeated Invaders Aftercare Kit*, followed by the instructions '(a) Sleep Well' and '(b) Don't Call Again'.

With a hydraulic hiss and a wheezing of steam pistons, the castle rose up on four gigantic mechanical legs and began to march across the landscape. In a matter of moments, the entire pearl-white edifice had plodded over the horizon and disappeared.

Randalf rolled on to his side and snuggled into his pillow. Next to him

16

Ella and Edward gently snored, while Norbert's shoulders slowly rose and fell as he sucked his thumb.

'Mummy,' he murmured contentedly.

'I say, you there!' came a querulous voice. 'Yes, you. With the budgie.'

Joe looked up from the dusty flagstones. As the drawbridge had risen he'd been pitched into the castle and now found himself lying in the middle of a courtyard. Veronica had just landed on his shoulder.

'Has the castle repelled the invaders?' the querulous voice enquired.

A tall, thin, balding man with silver-rimmed spectacles and a long flowing robe edged with white ermine came hurrying towards Joe and Veronica from the opposite side of the courtyard. A fat black Labrador padded along behind him, panting heavily.

'Invaders?' said Joe, climbing to his feet.

The man strode over to one of the arrow-slits in the wall and peered out. 'Ah, yes, seems it has. Sleeping like babies. Mechanical castle, one; invaders, nil. Well done, Whatever! Jolly good show.' As the castle began to judder and lurch alarmingly, he turned to Joe and stuck out a hand. 'Lord Asbow,' he said, pumping Joe's arm up and down. 'You must be the new man in Experimental Woodwork. Fluffy, is it? No, that was the last one . . .'

Beside him, the fat Labrador broke wind loudly.

'Joe,' said Joe, trying to ignore the appalling smell. 'Joe Jefferson.'

'Good to have you on board,

18

Jefferson,' said Lord Asbow. 'I say, what a splendid pet,' he added, and nodded at Veronica. 'Beautiful plumage.' He patted the Labrador's shoulders. 'Why don't you two join me and Daemian here in the Senior Common Room for a nice cup of dust?'

Veronica winked at Joe, who nodded uncertainly. He looked around, but there was no sign of the lamp-post. This strange person seemed to have mistaken him for someone else, but at least he seemed friendly. The castle gave another lurch. The whole place appeared to be moving.

'Yes, errm, thank you,' said Joe. 'We'd love to, but . . .'

'Excellent,' said Lord Asbow, taking him by the arm and propelling him across the courtyard, through a door and into the first of a maze of corridors. They turned right, then left, then left again, then climbed a flight of stairs, then descended another flight of stairs and turned left again . . .

'Oh, you'll soon get the hang of the place,' said Lord Asbow airily as he saw the look of confusion on Joe's face. 'And until you do, I'm happy to show you around.'

They came to a tall whitewashed door, bearing the sign *Senior Common Room Door—Instructions for Use*, followed by a column of tiny writing, numbered 1 to 37. Seizing the handle, Lord Asbow opened the door with a flourish and ushered Joe and Veronica inside.

The Senior Common Room of the University of Whatever was full of balding professors wearing silver-rimmed spectacles and long, flowing ermine-edged robes just like Lord Asbow's. Each of them had a different pet. There was a pink-eyed mouse, a neurotic looking gerbil, a guinea pig that was losing its fur, a plump duck, a tortoise with *Daemian* written on its shell in white paint, and a small goldfish in a glass bowl.

Lord Asbow removed an ermine-edged gown from a hook behind the door and handed it to Joe.

'Here, try this one on for size, Jefferson,' he said, 'and let's see about that cup of dust.' He looked up. 'I say, Mrs Couldn't-Possibly, two cups of your finest dust, if you'd be so kind.'

A tall, elegant woman with clear blue eyes and silky blonde hair the colour of sun-ripened barley came sashaying across the room. She stumbled slightly as the sleepy-looking wombat following her stepped on the hem of her silk dress. 'Certainly, Lord Asbow,' she said with a smile.

She turned to a pair of silver pot-bellied urns that stood on a sturdy oak sideboard beneath a complicated diagram covered in arrows and annotations. She held a bone-china cup beneath the first urn's spout and turned the tap. Dust trickled into the cup like the sands of an upturned egg-timer. She turned

21

to the second urn and added boiling water, then repeated the process with the second cup. With a gently steaming cup of dust in each hand she returned to Lord Asbow and Joe, almost tripping over her sleepy wombat as she did so.

'Oh, Daemian,' she chided, 'do try not to get under my feet.'

'Thank you so much,' said Lord Asbow.

'My pleasure,' said Mrs Couldn't-Possibly. 'I vacuumed it up fresh this morning from the roof of the west tower. Finest sunrise dust.'

'Mmm, delicious,' said Lord Asbow, as the fat Labrador at his side began licking the sleepy wombat's face. 'Daemian! Leave Daemian alone!' Lord Asbow scolded, prodding his Labrador with his foot. The appalling smell returned. He went over to a battered-looking leather sofa on which a balding professor with silver-rimmed glasses and long robes was sitting, a goldfish bowl beside him. 'If you wouldn't mind moving your pet, Professor Quedgely.'

'Yes, Lord Asbow. Sorry, Lord Asbow,' the professor said, picking up the glass bowl and climbing to his feet. 'Come on, Daemian,' he said, gazing fondly at the goldfish swimming round lethargically in the green-tinged bowl, 'time to change your water.'

Lord Asbow sat down on the sofa and patted the cushion next to him. 'Take the weight off your feet, Jefferson.'

On Joe's shoulder, Veronica leaned across and whispered in his ear. 'I think we've got them fooled. Just remember to call me Daemian while I think of a way to get us out of here.'

Joe nodded and sat down next to Lord Asbow. He took a sip from the cup. The pale greenish liquid tasted delicious—sweet and fizzy and full of strange and wonderful flavours that Joe had never tasted before. He drained the cup in one go. He felt wide awake and full of energy.

'Real pick-me-up, sunrise dust,' said Lord Asbow. 'Unlike sunset dust, which can make you sleep for a week. Especially if you don't dilute it . . . Ah,

I see you're admiring the portrait of our founder,' he said, following Joe's gaze.

The wood-panelled wall on the opposite side of the Common Room was covered with gold-framed portraits of all shapes and sizes. There was a square painting of a red-faced professor with a plump piglet tucked under one arm, and a tall thin painting of a worried-looking professor clutching a hefty python, while between the two of them was an oval-shaped painting of a short-sighted professor wearing thick glasses and with a speckled hen perched on his head . . . But what had caught Joe's eye was the large opulently framed portrait that had pride of place above the mantelpiece.

It showed a portly individual in a bottle-green bowler hat and an oversized orange suit with a garish red check. The large yellow daffodil in the buttonhole of his lapel was squirting a jet of water, while his flamboyant bow-tie appeared to be revolving. In one hand was a glowing lantern; in the

VLAD THE TICKLER

other, a pink feather-duster.

'Vlad the Tickler,' said Lord Asbow proudly. 'A fascinating character. He arrived here quite unexpectedly through a portal . . . Do you know what portals are, Jefferson?'

'Well, actually . . .' Joe began.

'Let me tell you,' Lord Asbow continued without a pause. 'Awkward blighters, portals. Things fall into them, things fall out of them. And all quite without warning. One of those things just happened to be our illustrious founder. Muddle only knows where *he* came from, but he was a real eccentric. His hobby was tickling people,' said Lord Asbow, pointing at the pink feather-duster in Vlad the Tickler's hand.

'But he was very popular in Muddle Earth,' he went on. 'And he must have liked it here because he stayed, and fell in love with a barbarian princess, Heidi the Gorgeous, and built this mechanical castle for her.' Lord Asbow pointed at Vlad's other hand. 'He was carrying that lantern when he first stumbled through the portal. He put it down on the soil on this side, and the next thing he knew, it had grown into a splendid lamp-post . . .'

'Lamp-post!' Joe exclaimed, nearly dropping his teacup.

'Yes,' said Lord Asbow matter-of-factly. 'A rather jolly little *walking* lamp-post. Because it grew in the magic earth at the entrance to the portal, the lamp-post and the portal are linked. Wherever the lamp-post goes, the portal follows. And as I said, they're awkward blighters, portals. Spoilt children are forever dropping out of them, putting on crowns and calling themselves kings and queens . . . It's all such a dreadful bore!'

'I've seen the lamp-post,' said Joe excitedly. 'It's somewhere in the castle.'

'Is it?' said Lord Asbow with a sigh. 'That means the portal's here too. Take my advice, Jefferson, and watch your step. Last time the portal was here, your predecessor allowed one of his most remarkable inventions to fall into it. It was unforgivably careless of him!' Lord Asbow frowned. 'He left us no choice but to impose the harshest punishment of all. We separated him from his pet, Daemian the hamster, and expelled him from the university. And you know what that means,' he said darkly.

'I do?' said Joe.

'Separated from our pets, Jefferson, we are condemned to become werecreatures every triple full moon. Werebudgies, werelabradors, wereducks, weregoldfish, and in Fluffy's case, a werehamster. No, Mr Fluffy had only himself to blame.' He shrugged. 'Goodness knows where he is now.'

'I think I might know,' Joe muttered under his breath.

Lord Asbow's eyes took on a faraway look. 'Mr Fluffy's flat-pack wardrobe!' he breathed. 'An extraordinary, wondrous thing. Just think of it, Jefferson, an entire wardrobe, but in pieces and packed into a cardboard box as flat as a barbarian's pancake, together with the most detailed instructions ever devised. And a handy little tool to put it together.' Lord Asbow shook his head. 'All lost in a moment down that wretched portal.

Goodness knows where it went.'

'I think I might know,' Joe muttered a second time.

'What's that, Jefferson?'

'Nothing,' said Joe, climbing to his feet and stepping over Lord Asbow's panting Labrador. He crossed the room to the portrait and peered closely at a shadowy figure in the background. It was Edward Gorgeous.

'That's Vlad the Tickler's nephew, Edward,' said Lord Asbow, who had followed him across the room, together with his decidedly smelly Labrador. 'History doesn't record what happened to him . . .'

'I think I might know,' Joe muttered for the third time.

'. . . unlike his uncle,' Lord Asbow went on, 'who lived to a ripe old age and founded this university. But shortly afterwards he was accidently trodden on by the building when somebody pulled the wrong lever. Ever since then, we at the University of Whatever have devoted ourselves to the discussion, study and writing of instruction sheets and manuals for absolutely everything,

29

whatever it is, so that no such mistake should ever be made again.'

Lord Asbow laid a hand on Joe's shoulder as his fat Labrador broke wind once again. Veronica dived for cover inside Joe's robes, while Joe held his nose and tried not to breathe.

'But enough of all this, Jefferson,' said Lord Asbow. 'Let me show you to your woodwork laboratory.' He paused and sniffed the air. 'What on Muddle Earth is that smell?'

'I think I might know,' said Joe.

Multi-Stepped Circular Elevation Structure, the notice read. *Instructions for use: (a) Hold handrail securely and place right foot on first step. (b) Place left foot on second step. (c) Place right foot on third step . . .*

Joe shook his head as he followed Lord Asbow up the spiral staircase. Everything in the castle—from doorknobs to window catches, bell pulls to banisters—seemed to have a notice attached to it, with ridiculously detailed instructions. And try as he might, Joe couldn't stop himself from reading them, no matter how pointless they turned out to be.

Veronica's head poked out from the folds of Joe's robes. 'Where are we?'

31

she whispered.

'Climbing a multi-stepped circular elevation structure,' Joe whispered back. 'To the top of one of the towers.'

'Here we are,' announced Lord Asbow brightly as beside him Daemian the Labrador wagged his tail and looked up expectantly at the door in front of them, which bore the notice *Experimental Woodwork*. Lord Asbow threw open the door and ushered Joe inside. 'I'll leave you to it, Jefferson, old chap. Make yourself at home. If you need anything, I'll be in the Senior Common Room,' he said, turning on his heels and heading back down the staircase, followed by Daemian. 'You know where to find it,' his voice floated back. 'Down the stairs, second left, third right, fourth left, eighth right, right again, left again, right again . . .'

Joe looked around. He was standing in a cluttered workshop. Strange, unlikely-looking woodwork tools lay scattered across low, squat workbenches. There were crocodile saws and three-headed hammers, corkscrew mallets and duck-billed pliers, musical chisels, steam-driven drills and a humpback sanding machine that slouched in the corner. The walls were papered with complicated diagrams of wardrobes and cupboards and chests of drawers, while the floor was strewn with sawdust and wood-shavings. A small golden hamster popped its head up out of the wood-shavings and fixed Joe with a beady-eyed stare. The next moment it shot across the workshop, through Joe's legs and out through the open door.

'Blast! You've let the hamster out!' said a portly professor with a manky grey parrot perched on his shoulder. He stepped into the workshop. 'The name's Munderfield,' he said, 'the new experimental woodwork professor.

33

And you are?'

'Jefferson,' said Joe. 'The experimental . . . errm . . . errm . . . instruction-notice professor!'

'Oh, really?' said Professor Munderfield. 'Jolly good show. And don't worry about the hamster. I'm sure it'll find its own way back. Separated from its owner, poor thing. Bad business. Perhaps you've heard about it?'

'Yes, I have,' said Joe, edging towards the door. 'It's awful. I couldn't imagine being separated from Daemian here,' he added, tickling Veronica under her beak.

Veronica nodded theatrically.

'Yes,' said Professor Munderfield uncertainly, as he pulled a handkerchief from the pocket of his robes and wiped fresh parrot droppings from his lapel. 'I couldn't imagine it either.'

Joe backed out of the door and headed down the stairs.

'I don't think he suspected anything,' said Veronica. They reached the bottom of the staircase. 'Now, which

34

way shall we go?'

'Let's try this way,' said Joe, turning to the right and setting off along a dimly lit corridor.

He took a left turn, then a right turn. Then another right turn . . . He found himself in a small courtyard and looked up. Above him were crenellated battlements, with stone steps leading up to them. Above the battlements, the ivory towers of the university rose up.

'This place is weird, even for Muddle Earth,' said Joe.

'You can say that again,' said Veronica. 'The rest of us stay as far away from it as we can. Which isn't always easy, with the whole place travelling around the way it does. And it attracts the weirdest types, who seem to like it here. Thumb-sucking vampires. Pet-loving werepeople. Zumbies. Poltergeese. Black bunnies called Binky . . . And you just went rushing inside, Joe, before Randalf or I could stop you.'

'I know. I'm sorry,' Joe said apologetically, 'but I saw—' he pointed —'*that*!'

35

The lamp-post had just appeared. There it was above them, skipping merrily along the battlements. Its light twinkled brightly as it broke into a little tap dance.

'Wait! Stop!' Joe shouted. He bounded up the stone steps that led to the battlements, two at a time. 'Come back!'

The lamp-post reached the end of the walkway and leaped across to the roof of the nearest tower.

'Careful, Joe,' warned Veronica, taking to the wing as Joe sprinted along the battlements, his ermine-edged robes flapping.

He launched himself into the air after the lamp-post,

36

and landed on the top of the tower just as the moving castle lurched to one side.

'Whoooaah!' Joe cried out with alarm, sliding down the roof-tiles towards the edge of the tower.

A hand shot out, seized the hem of his robes and hauled him back from the brink. Joe looked up. Mrs Couldn't-Possibly was smiling down at him. She was wearing a floral-patterned pinafore, a pair of ermine-edged rubber gloves and a mask, which she had pulled aside. Next to her stood a large upright vacuum cleaner, a sleepy-looking wombat draped round its handle.

'Careful there, Professor Jefferson,' she said, helping him to his feet. 'Turret-jumping can be dangerous when the castle's on the move. Didn't you see the notice?'

The castle was lumbering over a rocky landscape of cliffs and crags on its huge mechanical legs. *Clunk! Clunk! Clunk!* Its footfalls echoed through the Here-Be-Dragons Mountains as its walls trembled and its turrets swayed.

37

Behind Mrs Couldn't-Possibly, the lamp-post did a little somersault and jumped on to the adjacent tower. The air around it seemed to ripple and there came the sound of distant voices.

'Joe! Ella! Time for lunch!' It was Joe's dad's voice. 'Honestly, where have those two got to?'

'Don't ask us!' the twins called back. 'We haven't seen them anywhere.'

It was the portal back to his world. Joe felt a pang of homesickness in the pit of his stomach. He had to admit he'd had fun in Muddle Earth, what with the broomball match and the cake-baking competition, and helping Randalf. But, it seemed, life was continuing back home without him— his parents were back, the twins had been let in, lunch was ready and on the table . . . If only he could get the lamp-post to stop and listen, then perhaps it would come with him, and he and Ella could finally get back to where they belonged.

'I was just doing a spot of vacuuming,' Mrs Couldn't-Possibly was saying. 'Sunrise dust gathers on the east sides of the towers,' she explained. 'Sunset dust gathers on the west . . .'

But Joe wasn't listening.

'Come back, *please!*' he shouted as he threw himself after the lamp-post and landed on the top of the next tower in a cloud of dust.

'Careful, Professor Jefferson!' shouted Mrs Couldn't-Possibly. 'That's the *west* side! *Sunset* dust!'

Too late. Joe breathed in the twinkling particles and instantly fell asleep.

'Joe!' Veronica squawked as Joe fell from the tower and tumbled through the air. 'Joe!'

'Hello, clouds! Hello, mountains!' trilled the young dragon as he flapped his wings and flew across the sky. He swooped down lower and landed beside a mountain lake. 'Hello, flowers!' he said, thin wisps of smoke curling from his nostrils.

Eraguff the eager-to-please dragon carefully picked the tiny mountain blooms, some white, some pink, some pale yellow, that were growing in the rocky cracks and crevices. When he had gathered a small bunch, he raised it to his nose and sniffed their delicate fragrance.

'Atishoo!'

A jet of flame shot from his nostrils and instantly incinerated the pretty flowers.

'Oh dear! Not again!' said Eraguff, dropping the blackened remains of the bouquet. 'Sorry, flowers. Silly me.'

Just then, a solitary green-scaled dragon with flame-red wings and a sinuous tail of copper and bronze came gliding into view. Eraguff looked up and waved.

'Coo-ee! Uncle Alan! It's me, Eraguff! Isn't it a beautiful morning? I was just picking some flowers for my nest. They do brighten the place up, don't you think? And they're *so* pretty. Though I have to be careful, what with my allergies . . . Uncle Alan? Uncle Alan? Can't you stop, Uncle Alan? . . .'

He lowered his hand and his shoulders slumped. 'Oh, obviously not.'

Eraguff blew a sad little smoke ring out of the corner of his mouth as, studiously ignoring him, the green-scaled dragon flew past on his majestic red wings.

'Likes to keep himself to himself, does Uncle Alan,' called Eraguff to a purple dragon that was just passing overhead. 'Coo-ee! Miss Dragonbreath. It's me, Eraguff!'

'We all do,' said the purple dragon sternly as she continued on her way.

Eraguff sighed. 'Oh, well,' he said to no one in particular. 'I might as well go and tidy my nest.'

With a flap of his beige wings, the young dragon took to the air, his grey scales drab and dull in the early morning sunshine.

'Goodbye, flowers! Goodbye, lake!' he trilled as he headed off towards a nearby mountain top.

Two minutes later, he spiralled down out of the sky and landed lightly on a messy collection of stubby branches, tangled twigs and tattered scraps of

41

material that was balanced precariously on the top of a high rocky crag. Folding his wings and coiling his tail, Eraguff settled himself down and began tidying the nest. After half an hour, every single branch, twig and scrap of material had been carefully rearranged.

The nest looked exactly the same.

'That's better,' said Eraguff.

He picked up a pair of antique knitting needles and turned to the balls of wool, yarn and twine in his collection, all of them made by unravelling the threads of scrap material: abandoned curtains from Goblintown, discarded vegetable sacks from Trollbridge, mislaid snuggly-wugglies from the Ogre Hills, yak-wool duvets from Nowhere . . . in fact anything that had blown off a washing line, fallen from a passing cart or been accidently left by a mountain lake; Eraguff swooped on them all—so long as they were bright and colourful.

Humming a cheerful little tune, Eraguff selected a ball of cerise sisal and resumed knitting the endless stripy scarf that filled the centre of his nest in multicoloured coils. *Click-clack, clickety-clack* went the knitting needles.

'*Binky the Bunny, Binky the Bunny,*' he sang. '*He's big and black, and loves his honey . . .*'

CLUNK! CLUNK! CLUNK!

Eraguff stopped knitting and looked up as a shadow fell across his nest. It was that castle again, picking its way through the Here-Be-Dragons Mountains.

'Hello, castle!' Eraguff trilled.

As the castle rocked and swayed from side to side, a tiny figure fell from the top of a tall tower and came tumbling down through the air . . .

. . . and landed in the soft coils of Eraguff's

knitted scarf.

CLUNK! Clunk! Clunk!

The castle stomped off into the distance, over the mountain tops and far away.

Eraguff looked down. 'Hello . . . whatever you are,' he said.

'*Zzzzzzzzzzz*,' came Joe's reply.

Joe yawned and stretched, then looked about him. He was high up, with an unbroken view of mountains stretching away in all directions as far as the eye could see.

'Where am I?' he mumbled sleepily.

He was tangled up in what appeared to be an enormous woolly scarf at the centre of a mess of twigs and branches.

'In my nest,' came a voice from above, 'in the Here-Be-Dragons Mountains.'

Joe looked up to see a large dragon with dull grey scales and dingy beige wings swoop down and land on the edge of the nest.

'And I must say it's lovely to have visitors.'

45

'Is it?' said Joe.

'Oh, yes,' said the dragon. 'You've no idea how lonely it can get up here in the mountains. Thank you so much for dropping in.'

'Dropping in?' said Joe.

'Yes, you fell off that moving castle of yours. You must be a professor,' he said, nodding at Joe's ermine-edged robes. 'Lovely material, by the way.'

'Yes,' said Joe, puzzled, as he looked down at the clothes he was wearing. 'I . . . I must be.'

His head felt as if it had been packed full of cotton wool and he was finding it difficult to collect his thoughts.

'My name's Eraguff,' said the dragon. 'What's yours?'

Joe frowned. What *was* his name? Joshua? No, that didn't sound right . . . Jeremy? Julian? . . . *Joe*. Yes, that was it.

'Joe,' he said.

'Delighted to meet you, Joe!' exclaimed Eraguff. 'Can we be friends? Can we? *Can* we?'

'Yes, I suppose so,' said Joe, trying to concentrate.

46

'We can pick flowers and paddle in the lake and roll up balls of wool,' the dragon gushed. 'And I can take you for a ride on my back! Oh, we're going to have such fun!'

'Yes, but first,' said Joe, 'there's something I have to do . . . At least, I think there is. But I can't quite remember what.' He scratched his head. 'I'm trying to get back home . . . That much I do remember, but I can't remember where home *is*!'

'The moving castle?' suggested Eraguff.

'No, not the castle,' said Joe. What was wrong with him? He still felt so sleepy. He yawned. 'But I'd know it if I saw it,' he said. 'I'm sure I would.'

'Then climb aboard,' said Eraguff, eager to please. He crouched down and spread his beige-coloured wings wide. 'And we'll see if we can jog that memory of yours!'

Joe jumped to his feet and scrambled on to the dragon's back.

'That's it,' said Eraguff. 'Now, hold tight and try not to worry . . .'

'Worry about what?' said Joe as

Eraguff flapped his wings and took to the air.

'Oh, nothing really,' said Eraguff cheerfully as he wobbled alarmingly from side to side. 'It's just that I've never actually taken anyone for a ride on my back before. And I dare say it'll take a bit of getting used to.'

The dragon swooped down unsteadily, before soaring back into the air on trembling wings. Still wobbling, he made his ungainly way across the sky, while Joe clung on for all he was worth.

'This is fun, isn't it?' Eraguff called back.

'It is?' said Joe.

All at once, a gust of wind caught the dragon and sent him hurtling off towards a nearby mountain top in a flurry of flapping wings and billowing smoke. At the last moment, just as Joe was certain they were going to crash, Eraguff managed to steady himself and clear the jagged top of the mountain with inches to spare. On the other side, the dragon glided down and landed on a narrow ledge in front of a cave entrance.

'Phew, that was close,' said Eraguff, a couple of small smoke rings rising from his nostrils. 'But I think I'm getting the hang of it.'

'Do you mind keeping the noise down,' boomed a voice from inside the cave. 'Some of us are trying to sleep on our treasure hoards.'

The large, disgruntled head of a green-scaled dragon emerged from the cave and blinked twice.

'Uncle Alan!' trilled Eraguff.

'Oh, it's you,' said Uncle Alan

grumpily. 'I might have known.' His eyes narrowed. 'And what on Muddle Earth have you got on your back?'

'This is Joe,' said Eraguff proudly. 'He's my friend.'

'Friend?' said Uncle Alan, eyeing Joe. 'You mean you're not going to eat him?'

'*Eat* him?' said Eraguff. 'Of course not.'

'Then you won't mind if I do,' said Uncle Alan, licking his lips.

'I think it's time to leave,' said Eraguff quickly, and launched himself back into the air.

Beating his wings as fast as he could, the dragon flew off across the mountains, leaving Uncle Alan at the cave entrance behind them, grumbling about being woken up by foolish nephews who played with their food.

'Don't mind Uncle Alan, Joe,' said Eraguff. 'I'm sure he didn't mean it.'

They flew on, high above the mountains and out across the dusty plains beyond. In the distance, Mount Boom and the Musty Mountains came into view, and far beyond that the surface of the Enchanted Lake glittered in the warm sunshine.

Eager to please as ever, Eraguff called back over his shoulder. 'Are you all right back there, Joe?' he said. 'Sitting comfortably? Now, you just give a shout if anything jogs your memory.'

The morning sunlight played on the turrets and spires of Stinkyhogs School of Wizardry, casting long shadows across the empty courtyards and deserted broomball pitches. The corridors were quiet, the carpetless staircase was still, while the sound of silence was deafening in the classrooms, dormitories and halls. No goblin grumbles, no barbarian maiden giggles, no *pitter-patter* of massive ogre feet or *rumble-gurgle* of troll tummies. It was the school holidays and nothing was stirring, not even a mouse . . .

Except, that is, for Mr Fluffy,

who had just emerged from his nest of shredded exam papers in the corner of the teachers' room. Nose twitching and little  eyes twinkling behind steel-framed spectacles, Stinkyhogs's woodwork teacher trotted over to the window and looked out. In the courtyard below stood the wooden hamster wheel, its rungs worn and scratched from heavy use.

'Phew,' he sighed. 'I'm glad that's over . . .' Mr Fluffy removed the stubby pencil from behind his ear and pulled a small leatherbound diary from his tweed jacket. He thumbed through its pages, looking for the next likely triple full moon and put large question marks against several dates. '. . . for now,' he said darkly.

He turned away from the window and surveyed the roomful of empty armchairs. With a little sigh, he selected one and slumped down into it, lost in thought. So lost in thought, in fact, that he didn't notice the dingy dragon through the window, circling high in the sky, flapping its beige wings and wobbling unsteadily as a figure clung to its back.

The seven brightly painted houseboats bobbed about on the Enchanted Lake. There was a half-timbered mansion, a white-stucco villa, a bungalow with portholes, a log cabin, a thatched cottage, a tin shack and an elegant town house, each one perched in its own wooden hull.

'Morning, Melvyn,' called Ernie the Shrivelled, throwing open one of the lattice windows of his thatched cottage and sticking his head out.

He waved to the flamboyant wizard in the mauve robes who had just sashayed through the doorway of the white-stucco villa and was swanning about on the deck.

'Morning, Ernie,' he called back.

'Morning, Bertram. Morning, Boris.'

Bertram the Incredibly Hairy in the log cabin and his brother, Boris the Bald, in the tin shack waved back from their windows.

'Morning,' called Eric the Mottled from the top storey of his half-timbered mansion. 'Morning, Roger. Morning . . . errm . . . errm . . .'

'Morning,' sighed Colin the Nondescript, and pulled his head back through the porthole of his bungalow.

On the deck of his elegant town-house boat, Roger the Wrinkled, head wizard of Muddle Earth, blew on his freshly varnished nails.

'Hmm . . . I'm not sure that black suits me,' he mused. 'But I'm a slave to fashion.' He adjusted his leopard-print dressing gown as he lay back in his deckchair and kicked off his shiny red patent leather court-shoes. The shoes were certainly eye-catching, but they did give him such terrible blisters. The last time he'd worn them, he remembered, was at the Goblet of Porridge broomball match . . . Which reminded him, where *had* Randalf got

to? He'd promised to find the missing Goblet of Porridge and return with it. But that was ages ago. And since then, not a word. It really was very irritating.

Roger reached out and took a sugared bonbon from the little dish on the table next to him. He popped it in his mouth.

If Randalf didn't find the Goblet of Porridge soon, well, what choice did Roger have? As its most eminent wizard, not to mention ruler, Muddle Earth looked to him to set standards. No, there was really no question about it, mused Roger, reaching out for another bonbon. He would have to close Stinkyhogs School of Wizardry for good.

He settled back contentedly in his deckchair and closed his eyes—which was why he didn't see the dragon, high in the sky, circling the lake once, twice, three times, before flapping off in the direction of Elfwood.

In the depths of Elfwood, the talking trees of Giggle Glade kept silent and listened intently to the ancient tree shepherds in their midst, who were grumbling to each other.

'She's back,' creaked Mistletoe Mary.

'I didn't know she was away,' rustled Knotty Sue. 'What with those nasty little elves coming and going all hours of the day and night.'

''Ere comes one now,' grumbled Trev the Trunk.

'One hundred and eleven, one hundred and twelve, one hundred and thirteen . . .' squeaked the elf as it wandered past. 'Goggle, goggle, goggle.'

'Irritating creatures,' bristled Needles.

'She must have got back last night,' Mistletoe Mary was saying. 'I saw the lights on in that ridiculous gingerbread house of hers.'

There was the sound of rustling leaves as Lichen Larry folded his branch arms across his trunk. 'Well, all I can say is, Giggle Glade was a lot more peaceful before *she* moved in.'

Butch Canker and the Sawdust Kid nodded in agreement, dislodging several roosting batbirds as they did so.

'To be sure, to be sure,' agreed Mossback Murphy.

'Oh, listen to us lot,' said Bert Shiverwithers in a weatherbeaten voice as dry and tough as seasoned wood. 'We sound like a bunch of weeping willows. And we ain't!'

'No, we ain't!' came an orchard of voices.

'*We ain't beeches or birches or blackthorns,*' they sang out.

'*We ain't maple or poplar or lime; we ain't ashes or aspens, we ain't elms, we ain't oaks, we ain't chestnut or walnut or pine!*'

'So, what are we?' Bert Shiverwithers cried.

'*We're aints! We're aints! We're aints!*'

High over Elfwood, a dragon flapped slowly across the afternoon sky.

58

The warm afternoon sun shone down on the scented gardens of Golden Towers Finishing School for Little Princes and Princesses. Situated to the east of Goblintown in the gently rolling countryside of verdant hills and wooded dales, where there were definitely no dragons, Golden Towers prided itself on its wonderful grounds and gardens.

The little princes and princesses were in the middle of a game of emu croquet under the stern gaze of their teacher, Big Lady Fauntleroy.

'Hold your emu by the body, not the head, Prince Caspian,' she instructed. 'And Prince Adrian, aim at the armadillo, dear, not Prince Toby. That's the way . . .'

The princes and princesses were trying to hit their croquet balls, which were curled-up armadillos, with their mallets, which were emus, in order to send them rolling through hoops, which were hoops.

'And as for you girls,' their teacher said impatiently, her three chins trembling, 'stop gawping at the clouds and pay attention to the game . . .'

Princesses Camilla, Cecily, Guinevere and Araminta were staring up at the sky open-mouthed, while their emus wandered about, pecking at the camomile lawn in search of worms, and their armadillos snuffled into the rose bushes.

'But, Miss!' said Princess Araminta, pointing.

'I shan't tell you a second time,' warned Big Lady Fauntleroy.

On the terracotta terrace, the kings and queens of Golden Towers were taking afternoon tea.

'One lump or two?' said Queen Lucy.

'Three,' neighed the centaur in a black cummerbund and bow-tie.

Queen Lucy picked up three sugar lumps with the silver tongs and

60

fed them to the centaur.

'Thank you, your highness,' said the centaur, and placed a silver platter of cucumber sandwiches on the terracotta table.

'I've got some bad news,' said King Peter.

'Mfffll blcckmm?' mumbled King Edmund through a mouthful of cucumber sandwich.

'Worse than that, I'm afraid, Edmund,' said King Peter, shifting uneasily in his golden deckchair. He turned to Queen Susan and Queen Lucy, his face taut with foreboding. 'It's the lamp-post. It's escaped.'

'Escaped!' exclaimed Queen Susan.

'You mean it's fwee?' gasped Queen Lucy. 'Again! How fwightful!'

'Fllmmch!' spluttered King Edmund.

'It was Thragar Warspanner and his barbarian broomball team,' said King Peter with a shake of his head. 'We put them up in the east wing. Remember, Lucy?' he added accusingly.

'Well, we couldn't have had howwid barbawians in the main part of the castle,' Queen Lucy said defensively.

'Could we?'

'That's as may be,' said King Peter, 'but they've gone home now. The thing is, the east wing is where we locked up the lamp-post. I went down there this morning, only to find the trapdoor to the attic open. The lock had been broken. While they were here, one of the barbarians must have gone searching for plunder. You know what barbarians are like . . . The long and short of it is, the lamp-post has escaped. It's out there somewhere, wandering about—and you all know what *that* means!'

'The portal!' gasped Queen Susan. 'Out there, with the lamp-post . . . wandering about . . . But we could fall into it by accident and end up back—'

'I'm *never* going back!' burst out Queen Lucy defiantly, thumping the terracotta table with a little fist. 'Back to our old life—to that howwid old school with its howwid old teachers and its howwid old lessons . . . I'm a Queen of Golden Towers!' she sobbed, 'a beautiful faiwy-tale school that's just the way a school is meant to be.'

62

'There, there, Lucy, old thing,' said King Peter. 'Don't go upsetting yourself. We'll find that lamp-post and when we do . . .'

'Mwwbbl ffmmwwl bwllch!' said King Edmund, tossing his cucumber sandwich aside and helping himself to a handful of Turkish delight.

'That's right, Edmund,' said King Peter. 'We'll stomp all over it!'

'A dragon?' Big Lady Fauntleroy's imperious voice floated across from the camomile lawn. 'Where?'

'There, Miss,' came a chorus of princesses' voices.

Sure enough, high in the sky above Golden Towers Finishing School for Little Princes and Princesses, situated to the east of Goblintown in the gently rolling countryside of verdant hills and wooded dales, where there were definitely no dragons . . .

. . . was a dragon.

Eraguff and Joe had been flying all day. High over the Musty Mountains they had wobbled and dipped. Low over the Enchanted Lake they had spiralled and stuttered. Teetering and tottering, they had passed over the treetops of Elfwood and out across the Perfumed Bog beyond. Beneath the arches of Trollbridge and over the smoking towers of Goblintown, Eraguff had made his wobbly way, with Joe hanging on to his back for dear life. Finally, swooping round in a broad arc, they had narrowly avoided crashing into the high turrets of a golden castle, before heading back towards the wilderness of Nowhere.

And as they had flown, the effects of the sunset dust slowly wore off and Joe's head had begun to clear. By the time they were high over the barbarians' alpine valley, he was back to his old self.

'I say, what a splendid piece of cloth!' Eraguff exclaimed, spotting a duvet on the ground far below him. He flapped his wings so excitedly that he almost knocked Joe from his back. 'It could be just the thing for my nest.'

He swooped down for a closer look.

'Randalf! Norbert! Edward!' Joe cried out, seeing the sleeping figures in the alpine meadow below. 'Ella!'

The four of them were tucked up cosily beneath a plump duvet, their heads nestling on silk pillows. Eraguff came in to land next to the duvet with all the grace and poise of a stinky hog falling off a perfumed tussock. Joe climbed unsteadily from the dragon's back and shook the sleeping wizard by the shoulders.

'Those are *my* toffee apples!' spluttered Randalf, waking up with a start and sitting bolt upright.

Beside him, Edward, Ella and Norbert looked up sleepily from their pillows.

'Good evening, everyone,' Joe said. 'Time to get up!'

'I won't tell you again, Mum,' shouted Pesticide. 'Keep out of my bedroom!'

Pesticide the flower fairy stomped into her cavern bedroom and stormed over to the moss-covered table. Behind her, the ornately carved fairy-rune door slammed itself obediently shut.

'And *stay* out!'

Pesticide turned to the other fairies, who were seated at the table, and rolled her eyes.

'My mum's just as bad,' Nettle consoled her. 'She barged in and caught me painting my nails black last week and confiscated my nail varnish.'

'That's nothing!' said Thistle, her shock of purple hair bristling. 'When my dad found out I'd spray-painted my wings, he grounded me for a week!' She fluttered her translucent gossamer wings with their stencilled black skulls indignantly. 'I mean, what does he think *he* looks like, with those gaudy great butterfly wings of his and those rose-petal robes . . .' She smoothed down her tattered black tutu. 'That floral look is *so* over. But just try telling *him* that . . .'

'I know,' sympathized Briar-Rose, pouting as she touched up her black lipstick, 'but what can you expect from that lot? Lolling about on their flower beds, fussing over who gets to hold the hem of Queen Titania's gown, or which of them has the honour of pouring King Oberon's nectar . . . There's got to be more to life than that.'

'There is,' said Pesticide fiercely. 'There's a whole world out there just waiting for four flower fairies like us with the brains and talent to go and find what we want—and take it!'

All eyes turned to the moss-covered table where the Plant Pot of Power stood next to the Trowel of Turbulence.

'Two down and one to go,' said Pesticide, her intense green eyes glittering. 'Briar-Rose, remind me, what do we know about the Acorn of Abundance?'

Briar Rose turned to a wooden box that stood on a mahogany dressing table beside the ornate eight-poster bed, which was covered in lush flowering bindweed and creepers. Stamped on the front of the box, beside a small sliding door, were the words *Goggle Box*. Briar-Rose tapped on the lid with black fingernails and the door slid open. Two beady elf eyes peered out through the slit.

'So, what do we know about the Acorn of Abundance?' asked Briar-Rose.

'Flat, acorn-shaped and made of metal, the so-called Acorn of Abundance is one of the three enchanted objects of old old fairy magic that, once upon a time, were sold in a jumble sale and scattered to the three corners of Muddle Earth,' a squeaky elf voice told them. 'My enquiries have revealed that over the years the acorn has been used as a pastry-cutter, a door-wedge and a tool for removing the stones from centaurs' hoofs, before ending up in a goblin carpenter's toolbox. He found the acorn's flat shape was ideal for nestling in the palm of his hand and its stubby stem was perfect for tightening screws . . .'

'Yes, yes, a screwdriver,' said Briar-Rose. 'Get on with it!'

'Ahem.' The elf cleared its throat petulantly and continued. 'My further enquiries revealed that the acorn found its way into the Experimental Woodwork laboratory of the University of Whatever. There it was included as a tool in a flat-pack wardrobe which inadvertently fell through the portal marked by Vlad the Tickler's wandering lamp-post, which is currently back in Whatever Castle. So, if you want the acorn you'll have to break into the castle, find the lamp-post and go through the portal to Muddle only knows where. So there!'

The door slid shut.

'It's our biggest challenge so far,'

said Nettle.

Thistle nodded. 'Much harder than disguising ourselves as jeer-leaders to get into Stinkyhogs . . .'

'Or dressing up as a big barbarian baker to get into the Great Hall of Nowhere,' added Briar-Rose.

'You're right,' said Pesticide. 'It's not going to be easy, which is why we're going to need help.'

Just then, the ornately carved fairy runes on the door sparkled.

'There's an elf outside,' the door sang softly. 'Shall I let it in?'

Pesticide nodded and, with a click, the door unlocked itself and swung obediently open. The elf ran in.

'Goggle, goggle, goggle,' it squeaked as it gambolled over to the mahogany dressing table, opened the lid of the goggle box and jumped inside.

There was the sound of whispering and the sliding door at the front of the box slid open and a squeaky elf voice sounded.

'There are sixty-three and a half aints in Elfwood.'

Queen Titania glided down the curved marble staircase and into the vaulted throne room beneath Harmless Hill.

Above her head, Moth, Mustardseed, Cobweb and Peaseblossom fluttered and fussed, as they attended to her tall swaying hairdo. The queen's golden hair was piled high in a shimmering beehive, held in place with bramble combs and rose-thorn pins, and resplendent with interlaced garlands of peonies and sweet peas. Moth and Mustardseed were spraying clouds of pungent perfume over the backcombed tresses from small crystal bottles while, with little silver shears, Cobweb and Peaseblossom snipped and shaped the fern fronds and foliage that sprouted from the top.

On either side of Queen Titania, young Daisy and Dewdrop walked in step, fanning their queen with cabbage leaves. In front, Pollen skipped ahead, her gossamer wings quivering as she scattered rose petals in Queen Titania's path. Behind the queen, dainty Cloudburst and pretty Sprinkle watered the trailing grass train of her dress from tiny watering cans, while at the hem little Bluebell and Fuchsia took turns to carry it.

'Ron, my love. There you are,' Queen Titania cooed as King Oberon entered the throne room through a door at the opposite end.

Behind him, a scrum of brightly robed courtiers jostled for position at his shoulders. Each one clutched something different—a stool, a cushion, a goblet, a jug, a cheese and pickle sandwich—which they waved in the air.

'Take the weight off your feet, sir?'

'Nice comfy cushion?'

'Goblet of nectar, your highness?'

'Top you up, sir?'

'A bite to eat?'

'Tania,' said King Oberon, ignoring them. 'I made you this.'

He held up a pudgy fist as he strode towards his queen, his stained vest stretched tight across his wobbly belly.

'Oh, Ron!' she said, giving a melting

sigh. 'It's exquisite! The workmanship is divine! It's more dazzling than diamonds, more sumptuous than gold. Who needs rubies or emeralds when we have riches like these?'

'Thought you'd like it, love,' grunted King Oberon as he fastened the daisy chain he'd just made round Queen Titania's swan-like neck, before taking her by the hand and leading her towards their thrones.

Queen Titania sat down upon her garlanded throne of living willow wood while, next to her, King Oberon flopped into his leatherette reclining chair, as his courtiers extended the footrest and offered him his sandwich. Queen Titania's attendants fluttered prettily about her, several of the younger ones pulling lutes and recorders from the folds of their beautiful floral robes and beginning a lilting lullaby.

At that moment there was a rumbling sound from above, followed shortly after by a resounding *crash* that made the walls of the throne room tremble.

'Pesticide!' said Queen Titania in exasperation, her beehive hairdo swaying alarmingly. 'How many times have we told her not to slam the front door? And where can she be going *now*?'

'Search me, Tania, my love,' said King Oberon, scratching his belly.

'Oh, Ron,' Queen Titania wailed, and waved her hands towards the courtiers and attendants who were fluttering, fluffing, flapping and fussing tweely around them. 'Why, oh why, can't Pesticide be more like them?'

Pesticide, Thistle, Briar-Rose and Nettle flew up into the clear blue sky. Behind them, the front door to Harmless Hill, a great turf-covered slab of earth, hovered above the cavernous opening in the hillside. Turning in mid-air, her gossamer wings a blur of movement, Pesticide clapped her mittened hands together.

'Slam!' she commanded. The turf door came crashing down, sealing the entrance to Harmless Hill, its grass blending in seamlessly with that surrounding it. Pesticide giggled and turned to the others. 'It drives Mum and Dad wild when I do that,' she said.

'Oh, loooook,' gushed Thistle. 'A

baby stiltmouse. How sweeeeet.'

The others rolled their eyes. Below them on the crest of Harmless Hill, a small fluffy mouse with big blue eyes and extraordinarily long thin legs was tottering towards a daisy.

'Oh, no!' Thistle exclaimed. 'Watch out!'

She swooped down towards the baby stiltmouse as the daisy reared up and opened its gaping jaws, displaying a mouthful of savage fangs.

'Stop it, you naughty flower!' Thistle shouted as she landed between the stiltmouse and the killer daisy.

She pulled off a mitten and reached out her hand. But it was no ordinary fairy hand. It was green and covered in tiny needle-sharp prickles. The daisy hesitated, drool

77

dripping from its open mouth.

'I'm warning you,' Thistle told the flower sternly.

Behind her, the baby stiltmouse gave a little squeak, the killer daisy lunged and Thistle slapped the flower on the top of its petalled head.

'Stop it!' she commanded.

With a yelp of pain, the daisy shrank back and buried its head in its leaves, while the baby stiltmouse tottered over to the safety of its family mousehole.

'Come on, Thistle!' 'Stop mucking about!' 'We've got work to do!' the other flower fairies chorused.

'All right, sorry,' said Thistle, flying after the others as they set off across the sky. 'Oh, I wish I could have a sweet little baby stiltmouse of my own,' she said sadly, pulling her mitten back on, 'to pet and to stroke . . .'

The four flower fairies followed the road, past the Sandpit to their left and Trollbridge to their right, and over the Enchanted River. Flying on, Pesticide in the lead and the others following, they eventually came to a signpost at a fork in the road. The flower fairies landed beside it and looked up. There were three signs on the post pointing off in three different directions.

OGRE-HILLS—dusty, rocky, drab; I wouldn't go there if I were you, read the first.

TROLLBRIDGE—dirty, noisy, bustling; I wouldn't go there either, read the second.

ELFWOOD—absolutely enchanting place, full of trees. Go there! (In fact it's where I came from before they cut me down and turned me into this stupid signpost.)

Briar-Rose pulled off a mitten to reveal a hand that had five long curved thorns for fingernails. She crouched down and began carving her name into the wooden post, with skilful flourishes.

The other flower fairies exchanged meaningful looks.

'When you're quite finished, Briar-Rose,' said Pesticide testily, 'perhaps we can get on.' She glanced back at the signpost and pointed. 'Elfwood's that way.'

'Uh, yeah, sorry, guys,' said Briar-Rose, blushing. 'Sometimes I just can't

79

help myself . . .'

The others had already set off and, with a flap of her gossamer wings, she hurried after them.

'Briar-Rose,' she murmured sadly. 'Such a pretty name.' She sighed. 'For someone with such ugly fingers.'

They flew on, following the road as it skirted round the edge of the Perfumed Bog. To the south-west, shimmering in the afternoon sun, were the low, rounded humps of the Ogre Hills, while to the south-east, still no more than a distant smudge on the horizon, was the vast sprawling forest of Elfwood.

'I'm tired,' whined Nettle. 'My wings feel as though they're about to drop off.'

'Here we go again,' said Pesticide, frowning beneath her fringe of green hair. 'Nettle's complaining again. Honestly, Nettle, why are you always so *weedy*!'

Tears welled up in Nettle's eyes. 'I can't help it,' she said in a little voice. 'It's just the way I am.'

'All right, no need to cry about it,'

said Pesticide. 'I suppose it wouldn't hurt if we stopped for five minutes . . .'

'Oh, goodie,' said Nettle, cheering up. 'Look, there's the perfect spot, just there!'

Leaving the others, she flitted over to a pink hillock nearby, which was sticking up above the fragrant mud of the Perfumed Bog. She came fluttering down to land cross-legged on the ground.

'Aah, that's better,' she said, as she folded her wings behind her. 'But I'm so hot!'

Nettle pulled off her thick woolly mittens and leaned back. As her hands touched the surface of the pink hillock it trembled, and an almighty glugging squeal filled the perfumed air. The next moment, the hillock shot up into the air, sending Nettle sprawling in the mud.

'Wheeee! Wheeee! Wheeee! Wheeee!' came the anguished squeals as the most enormous pink stinky hog the flower fairies had ever seen went hurtling off across the Perfumed Bog.

'Well done, Nettle,' said Pesticide

sarcastically, hovering above her. 'When you've finished your little mudbath, we'll be on our way.'

Thistle and Briar-Rose sniggered.

Sitting up to her waist in the gloopy perfumed mud, Nettle stared down at her hands. The black nail varnish looked cool but could not disguise the nasty sting in her fingertips.

'It's not my fault,' she sobbed, pulling her mittens back on.

'There are sixty-three and a half aints in Elfwood,' said Pesticide, 'and we can't find a single one.'

She broke off a piece of cough-candy tile and popped it in her mouth.

The sun had been low in the sky when the four flower fairies had finally reached the fringes of Elfwood and entered the forest. They had begun their search as the shadows had lengthened, the sun had set and two of the three moons of Muddle Earth had risen up to take its place. Several hours later—and after endless frustrating conversations with the talking trees of Elfwood—Pesticide and her gang were no nearer to finding the aints than when they'd started. Finally, well past midnight, they had stumbled into a large glade with an eccentric gingerbread house at its centre.

Pesticide broke off another piece of cough-candy. A light came on, a spun-sugar window flew open and a head poked out.

'Who's that nibbling at my little house?' came a sing-song voice.

The head disappeared back inside.

'It's Miss Pinkwhistle,' spluttered Pesticide, nearly choking on the piece of cough-candy. She turned to the others. 'Just act normal. She'll never recognize us without our hoodies. Let me do the talking . . .'

A moment later there came the sound of a latch being lifted and Eudora Pinkwhistle, her hair in curlers and wearing a black nightdress, stepped out on to the liquorice veranda.

'What are you doing here?' she demanded, then paused. Her eyes widened as her gaze fell upon their gossamer wings. 'Why, but you're flower fairies!' She wagged a finger at Pesticide's companions. 'That windowsill is *not* for you, it's for the elves.'

'Sorry,' said Nettle, Thistle and Briar-Rose guiltily, dropping their pieces of gingerbread.

'It's stale anyway,' Nettle whispered to the others.

'Honestly, flower fairies,' Eudora muttered under her breath. 'So, why *are* you here?' she asked.

The four flower fairies exchanged looks. Pesticide stared down and shuffled her feet.

'Actually,' she began hesitantly, 'we've come to Elfwood to look for the aints.'

'The aints!' Eudora exclaimed and laughed extravagantly. 'Why, my dear little flower fairy, you don't mean to say you believe in *aints*? They're only to be found in fairy tales. But then again . . .' she added, with a condescending little giggle. 'I suppose you *are* fairies.'

Blushing furiously, the four flower fairies glared back at her. Eudora didn't notice.

'Aints,' she repeated, clasping her hands together and rising up on the balls of her feet. 'The tree shepherds of legend, forest keepers of myth, arboreal sentinels of the wild woods . . .'

Pesticide rolled her eyes. Thistle sighed. Briar-Rose examined her mittened hands.

'It's like being trapped in one of her lessons,' Nettle muttered.

'Shh!' hissed Pesticide sharply.

'According to fairy lore, the aints were a race of leaf-covered giants who looked after the trees of the forest,' Eudora went on, 'though if you ask me, they sound absolutely ghastly! Stomping around all day bossing saplings about and bullying bushes. Got far too big for their roots apparently and were told off by the fairy king and queen. Been sulking ever since, or so the fairy tales would have us believe— though as I say, *I* don't believe they ever existed in the first place.' She gave a tinkling laugh. 'So, you see, you've wasted your time coming to Elfwood. Now, run along, all of you. I'm sure it's well past your fairy bedtime. Your fairy mummies and daddies must be wondering where you are.'

'Well, *her* mum and dad are Queen Titania and King Oberon, so *she* can stay up as late as she likes,' Nettle piped up. She nudged Pesticide. 'Go on, tell her, Pesticide.'

'You mean, you're Ron and Tania's daughter!' Eudora went pale.

'Yeah,' said Pesticide sulkily. 'So what?'

'Oh . . . oh, nothing, my dear,' said Eudora. She smiled. 'Now, take a little piece of my house for your journey, and off you fly. And when you get back home you really shouldn't worry your parents about where you've been, or who you've seen,' she cooed. 'It can be our little secret.'

Pesticide shrugged and turned away.

'Come on, girls,' she said.

The four of them trooped back across the clearing and into the forest.

'Do you think she's right?' said Nettle glumly. She slumped down on a mossy bank and leaned back against a gnarled tree-trunk.

'You mean that it's all just a stupid fairy tale?' said Thistle, sitting down beside her. 'I dunno.'

Briar-Rose sent a pebble scudding over the forest floor with a moody kick of a clumpy black boot.

'But we looked it up on the inter-elf!' stormed Pesticide, 'so it *must* be true . . .'

She plonked herself down on the ground and hugged her knees to her chest. Briar-Rose sat down next to her.

'I mean, that old story that Peaseblossom, Cobweb, Moth and Mustardseed used to tell us, I never took it seriously,' she said. The others shook their heads in agreement. 'But then I got that goggle box, and the inter-elf said that the lost treasures of Harmless Hill really did exist.' Pesticide's green eyes gleamed.

'It said that the Plant Pot of Power was being used as a stupid old trophy for that ridiculous broomball game . . .'

'And it was,' said Nettle. Briar-Rose and Thistle nodded.

'It said that the Trowel of Turbulence was stuck in a mouldy old cake in the middle of Nowhere . . .'

'And it *was*!' the three of them chorused.

'The Acorn of Abundance—the most magical, the most magnificent, the most important of them all—is almost within our grasp.'

Pesticide looked up, her eyes blazing. 'And now this! No aints in Elfwood.' She hung her head. 'No aints anywhere.'

Pesticide climbed to her feet and began pacing back and forth, her mittened hands clasped behind her back.

'Oh, if only aints *did* exist. Just think what we could do together. With our brains and their brawn, we could unite the lost treasures of Harmless Hill once more, and if we did *that* . . . Just imagine!'

Pesticide flung her arms wide. Nettle, Thistle and Briar-Rose sprang up, their wings fluttering.

'We could rule the whole of Muddle Earth if we chose to!' said Pesticide. 'And the aints could keep everyone else in line—and they could be as bossy as they liked and *we* wouldn't tell them off,' she declared, carried away by the thought of it all. 'Not ever!'

'Feisty little thing, ain't she?' came a rustly voice.

'Talks a lot of sense,' said another. 'I like what she's been saying.'

'Almost reminds me of the old days . . .' sighed a third voice.

'Steady on,' cautioned a fourth. 'Let's not get carried away.'

'I agree with Trev, she does talk a lot of sense.'

'And certainly knows her old old fairy magic by the sound of it.'

'To be sure, to be sure.'

The four flower fairies looked around.

'It's the trees,' said Nettle wearily. 'They've got an opinion on everything . . .'

'Except when you ask them if they've seen any aints,' said Briar-Rose hotly. 'I bet if you asked that chestnut over there, it'd soon shut up. Or that elm. Or that oak . . .'

'I ain't a chestnut!'

'I ain't an elm!'

'And I ain't an oak!'

'And we ain't either!' came an orchard of voices.

'*We ain't beeches or birches or blackthorns,*'

they sang out. *'We ain't maple or poplar or lime; we ain't ashes or aspens, we ain't elms, we ain't oaks, we ain't chestnut or walnut or pine!'*

'So, what are we?' bellowed the oak tree that claimed not to be an oak tree.

'We're aints! We're aints! We're aints!' came the full-throated reply.

Pesticide took a little step backwards, her mouth open and eyes wide with astonishment. 'So you *do* exist . . . We've been looking for you all over Elfwood.' She frowned. 'Why didn't you tell us some of you were aints and not just trees?'

'Why should we?' said the aint who looked like an oak tree sulkily. 'That's no one's business but ours.'

His ivy-clad trunk was broad and gnarled, the bark thick and ridged with age. Two rheumy eyes stared down at Pesticide from deep-set canker-ridden knot-holes, and below them, plate-like fungus fringed the dark jagged opening that was his mouth. He folded two massive branch-like arms with a creak of wood and a rustle of leaves, sending dozens of small beetles scurrying for cover across the broad expanse of his chest.

'But why *wouldn't* a magnificent tree shepherd like you not want to make himself known?' Pesticide asked, fluttering her eyelashes. 'I mean, you're so distinguished-looking, if you don't mind me saying so.'

'Yes, well, I do what I can,' he said, his foliage trembling with pride. 'Try to stay in shape.' He lifted a great rooty foot, shook clods of earth from it, then stomped it down. 'You know. Running on the spot. Waving my branches about. That sort of thing . . . Mind you,' he added, with a twinge of discomfort, 'it's not easy. What with the ivy and the fungus, not to mention the beetles—ooh, they get right under my bark! Itch like mad, they do . . .'

'You poor thing,' said Pesticide, removing her mittens to reveal two elegant, long-fingered hands of chemical blue. 'Let me see what I can do.'

She reached out to the base of the aint's trunk and touched a stem of ivy that was growing there. The green leaves turned black, one after the other, spreading up the trunk and out on to the branches until every last clump of ivy had shrivelled and fallen to the ground.

'Ooh, that feels wonderful,' said the aint in astonishment.

'Now, how about that horrid fungus of yours?' said Pesticide. 'Lean closer.'

With a creaking and groaning, the aint brought his gnarled and knotty features close to Pesticide's outstretched fingers.

'And we'll see about that canker at the same time,' she said.

Her fingertips were a blur of blue as they fluttered over the aint's face and the fungus and the canker fell away.

'I haven't felt this good in years,' said the aint, straightening up.

'Now for the beetles,' said Pesticide triumphantly, tickling the aint's trunk-like tummy.

A shower of dead beetles fell from the thick ridged bark and tumbled to the forest floor below. The aint gave a deep groan of satisfaction.

'How can I ever thank you?' he said,

thrusting out a branch-like hand. 'Bert Shiverwithers at your service, leader of the Giggle Glade Mob.'

Around the flower fairies the aints came to life. They pulled their great rooty feet out of the ground, flexed their branch-like arms and nodded their leaf-covered heads in greeting as they introduced themselves.

'Lichen Larry,' wheezed an aint that looked like an old birch tree, his white bark mottled with thick brown and orange blotches. 'Ooh, thank you!' he exclaimed as Pesticide's blue fingertips banished the lichen from his bark.

'Mossback Murphy, my dear. Delighted to meet you,' said his neighbour, an aint who resembled an ancient hazelnut tree, his bark so thick with moss it looked like a green fur coat.

Pesticide's nimble fingers turned

the moss brown and the ancient aint shrugged it from his shoulders.

'Phew,' sighed Mossback Murphy. 'It was hot under that lot.'

Butch Canker and the Sawdust Kid introduced themselves next. They were a couple of elm-like aints in need of attention. Pesticide obliged, sending showers of elm-beetles falling from their trunks.

'Stone the crows, I feel like a young tree shepherd again,' said Butch Canker, his bark gleaming.

Mistletoe Mary and her friend Knotty Sue, who looked like beech trees, had bunches of mistletoe cleared from their limbs, while Trev the Trunk—who resembled a horse chestnut—was extremely glad to get rid of a bad case of toadstools. Needles, looking like a pine tree, had several hard-to-get-at nests taken care of, while Stumpy, who looked like a small Christmas tree, was relieved to say goodbye to a particularly stubborn squirrel who had taken up residence in a knot-hole.

The small grey pest had run off squealing when Thistle, Nettle and Briar Rose had removed their mittens and touched its bushy tail.

'Why, you lovely, lovely flower fairies, you,' said Fungus O'Foyle, a sycamore-like aint who had been patiently waiting his turn and was now being helped by all four flower fairies at once.

Pesticide took care of the fungus covering his bark, while Briar-Rose and Thistle pulled an old wasps' nest from his branches, and Nettle chased a woodpecker away.

The aints of the Giggle Glade Mob gathered round the flower fairies, their eyes aglow with gratitude and admiration.

'. . . Seven. Eight. Nine. Ten . . .' Pesticide counted, a blue finger pointing to the aints one after the other. 'Eleven,' she announced. 'So where are the other fifty-two and a half aints?'

'I have a sneaking suspicion *I'm* the half,' said Stumpy tetchily. 'Just wait till I catch up with that cheeky little inter-elf!'

'The other aints are in other parts of Elfwood,' Bert Shiverwithers informed Pesticide. 'There's the Babbling Brook Boys over by the babbling brook,' he said, with a wave of a branch-like arm. 'And the Dingly Dell Gang down in the dingly dell. And then there's the Wild Wood Crew.' He spread his branches wide. '*They're* all over the place.'

'They're mad, that lot!' nodded Lichen Larry approvingly.

'They certainly are,' said Bert Shiverwithers, 'and I'm sure they'd like to meet you, Pesticide. In fact all the gangs would. Stumpy, spread the word. We're calling a moonlight branch meeting.'

Stumpy stomped across to the nearest tree. 'Moonlight branch meeting,' he whispered out of the corner of his mouth. 'Giggle Glade. Pass it on.'

'Ooh,' said the tree. 'Did you hear that, Audrey? The aints are calling a moonlight branch meeting here in Giggle Glade. Pass it on.'

'Deirdre! I say, Deirdre!' Audrey called to her neighbour. 'A moonlight branch meeting. Giggle Glade. Pass it on.'

'Malcolm! Oh, Malcolm! Coo-ee! . . .'

The voices grew softer as the message was passed from tree to tree, spreading out to the farthest reaches of Elfwood.

A little while later, with the two full moons bathing the forest in dappled moonlight of purple and yellow, the ground beneath the flower fairies' feet began to tremble. *Stomp! Stomp! Stomp!* The heavy footfalls of tramping aints echoed through the forest.

'Mind out, Deirdre, here they come!'

'Watch out, Malcolm!'

The trees surrounding Giggle Glade began to shuffle out of the way, leaving broad avenues down which the approaching tree shepherds stomped. The first to arrive, down an avenue to the north, were the Babbling Brook Boys, a gang of stooped willow-like

99

aints with long trailing branches and gnarled straggly roots. Next came the Dingly Dell Gang, broad and stocky and covered in ivy, tramping into the glade from an avenue to the south. Finally, with the earth shaking and the forest trees swaying, the Wild Wood Crew burst on to the scene from all directions.

'Watch where you're going!'

'There's no need to shove!'

'An *excuse me* would be nice!'

The trees of Giggle Glade complained bitterly as the huge lumbering aints, tall and broad as ancient oaks, barged their way past them.

'So, what's this all about?' growled the leader of the Wild Wood Crew.

'Mad Marion,' said Bert Shiverwithers.

'Bert? Is that you?' said Mad Marion. 'Why, I hardly recognized you! You're looking so . . . handsome.'

'Meet my new friend, Pesticide,' said Bert, smiling broadly. 'She can do the same thing for you. Can't you, Pesticide?'

101

'It would be my pleasure,' said Pesticide, reaching out and withering the rash of mushrooms that sprouted from Mad Marion's trunk.

'And that's not all,' Bert went on, his voice becoming louder as he turned to the other aints. 'Pesticide and her friends have a plan. She says that with their brains and our brawn, we could rule the whole of Muddle Earth! We could boss everyone around as much as we liked,' he boomed. 'And they wouldn't tell us off. Not ever!'

'But what about Ron and Tania?' whispered one of the Babbling Brook Boys anxiously.

'King Oberon and Queen Titania are my parents,' Pesticide declared loftily, 'and they let me do whatever I want!'

'Oooooh!' went the aints, clearly impressed.

'Your days of sulking are over,' she told them. 'After all, why mope about here in Elfwood, allowing your roots to grow gnarled and your bark to become mossy? Why let the grass grow under your feet and the mistletoe clog your branches, when there's a great big world out there, just waiting to be bossed around? And with my help, you aints are just the ones to do it!'

She raised her arms high in the air and wiggled her chemical blue fingers.

'Today, Elfwood!' she cried. 'Tomorrow, Muddle Earth!!'

Her voice dropped. 'But first,' she said, her eyes narrowing beneath her fringe of green hair, 'there's something I want you to do for *me* . . .'

'Joe, it's you!' said Randalf, stifling a yawn. 'I was having the most extraordinary dream. I was being fed toffee apples by a pink stinky hog . . .'

He stopped, his eyes widening with alarm.

'Joe,' he whispered urgently. 'Don't move a muscle! There's a dragon right behind you, and it's staring straight at us . . .'

'Yes, I know,' Joe began.

'And it's a big one too! Huge, and mean-looking. And wild. Yes, wild, with horrible blood-red eyes! And it's drooling, Joe, out of the corner of its hideous twisted snout . . .'

'Oh, how rude!' exclaimed Eraguff. 'Joe, do you know these people?'

104

Joe turned and laughed. 'Yes, Eraguff, I do. Randalf, Norbert, and Edward here, are my friends. And this is Ella, my sister.' He patted the dragon on the neck. 'And *this*,' he said with a big smile, 'is Eraguff.'

'Your sister, did you say, Joe?' Eraguff took a step forward and extended a dull grey scaled hand. 'Enchanted to meet you, Ella.'

Ella threw the duvet aside and jumped back in alarm. Beside her Edward scrambled to his feet and stood protectively between her and the dragon. Norbert, meanwhile, had grabbed Randalf and was clutching him tightly to his chest.

'Can't . . . breathe . . .' gasped Randalf. 'Put . . . me . . . down . . .'

Eraguff looked hurt. 'I don't mean any harm,' he said. 'I only want to help. Anything I can do, just say the word. I'm always eager to please. Ask anyone . . .'

'That's right,' said Joe. 'Eraguff here has been extremely helpful from the moment I fell out of the University of Whatever . . .'

'You fell out of the University of Whatever?' said Randalf, struggling from Norbert's grasp and pushing the ogre away.

'Yes,' said Joe. 'Over the Here-Be-Dragons Mountains.'

'The Here-Be-Dragons Mountains?' said Randalf.

'Yes,' said Joe. 'And I landed in Eraguff's nest.'

'In Eraguff's nest?' said Randalf.

'Yes,' said Joe. 'Veronica and I were chasing the lamp-post . . .'

'The lamp-post?' said Ella.

'Veronica?' said Randalf. He frowned. 'And where is Veronica now?'

'So far as I know,' said Joe, 'she's still in Whatever. But I can't be certain. The lamp-post kicked sunset dust in my face and I fell asleep. That's when I toppled off the castle and landed in the nest.'

'That sunset dust of theirs is notorious,' Randalf agreed. 'I haven't slept so deeply in years.' He yawned expansively. 'I did try to warn you about the castle, Joe, but you just went rushing in. Terrible place, the

University of Whatever. Mr Fluffy told me all about it when I appointed him woodwork master at Stinkyhogs. The dons treated him quite disgracefully. Apparently, they threw him out over some silly little mix-up or other . . .' He clasped a hand to his brow. 'Oh, and poor, dear Veronica. To think of her, all alone in that terrible place!'

'We must find her, sir,' said Norbert, tears welling up in his triple eyes.

'*And* the lamp-post,' said Ella, clasping Edward by the hand and giving him a knowing look.

'Then it's agreed,' said Randalf. 'Our Goblet of Porridge quest will have to wait yet again. We must find the moving castle!' He turned to the rolled-up stair-carpet that lay half covered by the duvet. 'O woven conveyance of airborne

wondrousness, prepare for take-off, if you'd be so kind.'

The wizard tapped the carpet lightly with his staff, and with a little yawn, it unfurled, rose up and formed itself into steps. Eraguff gave an astonished gasp.

'Oh, but you're gorgeous!' he exclaimed, a flurry of smoke rings rising from his nostrils. 'Such quality! Such workmanship! Such rich colours!!'

'How sweet of you to notice,' the carpet breathed as it hovered in front of the drab grey dragon with the beige wings. 'It's so delightful to be admired.'

'Climb aboard, everyone!' Randalf interrupted, taking his seat on the top step of the flying carpet.

Norbert, Ella and Edward followed him.

'Come on, Joe,' said Ella, holding out a hand.

'I'll ride on Eraguff,' said Joe, turning to the dragon. 'If you'll have me.'

Eraguff's eyes glistened with emotion. 'You mean you'd rather ride on my back than on that exquisite tapestry?'

The stair-carpet cooed.

'I'd be honoured, Joe,' the dragon said. He paused as his eyes fell on the discarded duvet and pillows lying on the ground. 'And if nobody wants those,' he said, 'perhaps you could put them on my back. They'll make my scales more comfortable for you, and the material will look lovely in my nest . . . Though not as lovely as the beautiful tapestry,' Eraguff added.

The stair-carpet cooed again.

'Yes, well, if you're quite finished,' said Randalf from the top step, once Joe had arranged the duvet and pillows on the dragon's back, 'then perhaps we can get on.'

He tapped the stair-carpet which, with a little sigh, flew up into the air. At the same time, Eraguff beat his beige wings and took off.

'Now, where shall we start?' said Randalf.

'How about following those large moving-castle footprints down there?' Eraguff suggested helpfully.

'Ah, yes,' said Randalf, looking down at the muddy imprints in the grass of the alpine meadow far below, and the clumps of flattened trees that led through the wooded mountains beyond. 'Well done, that dragon!'

Eraguff beamed with delight and Joe had to cling on tightly as the dragon set off enthusiastically, the carpet following close behind.

'You might not be colourful,' said the stair-carpet, as they flew over the dusty plains of Nowhere, 'but you fly beautifully.'

'Thank you,' Eraguff replied, looking back and trying not to wobble. 'And so do you.'

On the top step of the stair-carpet, Randalf was already fast asleep. Further down the steps, Edward and Ella, locked together in deep whispered conversation, had eyes only for each other, while Norbert was busy examining the contents of his findy bag.

'Something from a barbarian's blouse,' he said, dropping a small yak-horn button into the bag. 'And something from a barbarian's pocket,' he said, adding a hairy gobstopper.

With the others occupied, and the dragon and the stair-carpet chatting happily, it was left to Joe to keep an eye on the trail of footprints on the ground below. But he too was having a hard time staying awake. The rolled-up duvet and pillows he was sitting on were so comfortable and the rhythmic beats of Eraguff's wings so hypnotic, that Joe's head was beginning to nod.

Flap! Flap! Flap!

'And I particularly like those little blue and yellow flowers in your border.'

'Oh, you noticed . . .'

Flap! Flap! Flap!

'And something pebbly from inside a barbarian's boot . . .'

Flap! Flap! Flap!

'It'll be OK, Edward, you'll see.'

'Will it, Ella? Will it?'

Flap! Flap! Flap!

Joe's chin came to rest on his chest. His eyes were closed and his breathing was steady.

Flap! Flap! . . .

WHUMPH!

Joe's eyes snapped open.

111

He was falling. Around him, the others were falling too.

Randalf, arms flailing and mouth opening and shutting like a surprised goldfish, was to Joe's left. Ella and Edward, clasped in a desperate embrace, were spiralling down through the air to his right, while just below them, Norbert tumbled over and over, as the contents of his findy bag scattered in all directions.

WHOOOSH!

A scaly hand caught Joe by the arm. Another grasped Norbert by the seat of his pants, while a coiled tail lassoed Edward and Ella.

'He-e-e-e-elp!' came Randalf's despairing cry as he disappeared into a cloud and out the other side, the ground hurtling up to meet him.

Swooping down, Eraguff lunged and caught the wizard in his jaws. Randalf found himself staring down a cavernous black tunnel fringed with jagged teeth.

'He-e-e-e-elp!'

Wobbling and weaving and tilting wildly from side to side, Eraguff flapped his beige wings for all he was worth. With all the elegance and agility of a stiltmouse dodging a killer daisy, the dragon came unsteadily in to land, his back legs pedalling furiously.

'Oof!' he grunted as his scaly belly struck the ground, and he skidded to a halt on the green turf.

'What happened?' gasped Joe. He felt the dragon's grip on his arm loosen.

'Mffll wppllf,' began Eraguff. He opened his mouth, and Randalf flopped on to the grass like a bedraggled lazybird that had just been rained on. 'Something flew into us,' Eraguff said, clearing his throat.

'Don't eat me,' Randalf whimpered weakly. 'Please don't eat me . . .'

'Eat you?' said Eraguff, looking hurt. 'I don't want to eat you. I just saved your life. And quite frankly, it's left me with a nasty taste in my mouth.'

The dragon uncoiled his tail and set Ella and Edward gently down, before releasing his grasp on the seat of Norbert's trousers.

'My findy things!' Norbert wailed, peering into his empty bag. 'Now I'll have to find new ones.'

'Honestly, Norbert, pull yourself together!' said Randalf, climbing to his feet with as much dignity as he could muster and wringing dragon drool from the hem of his robes. 'Nasty taste, indeed!' Randalf told the dragon. 'I'll have you know this cloak was fresh on last month.'

'Oh, oh, oh,' came a plaintive little voice from behind them.

Everyone turned to see the stair-carpet twisted up in knots and bulging in the middle like a python whose lunch had disagreed with it.

'You poor thing!' Eraguff exclaimed, rushing over and helping the carpet to unwind.

'Came out of nowhere!' it gasped. 'Black and flappy and shaped like a carpet sweeper!'

Disentangling itself, the stair-carpet rolled up tightly and scuttled behind the dragon on the tips of its tassels. There on the grass sat Eudora Pinkwhistle in a black cloak and

115

crumpled witch's hat, clutching her broom, Dyson, in one hand and a black leather satchel in the other.

'Well I never,' she said. 'Fancy bumping into you, headmaster.' She giggled girlishly. 'We really can't go on meeting like this.'

'Miss Pinkwhistle,' said Randalf. 'You really should look where you're going.'

'But headmaster,' said Eudora cheerfully, 'I could have sworn that you were asleep when we had our little accident.'

'Nonsense!' said Randalf. 'I'll have you know I was busy scanning the landscape for the giant footprints of Whatever Castle.'

'Oh,' said Eudora, clapping her hands together. 'How intriguing! Why ever were you doing that? Do tell.'

'Well, if you must know,' said Randalf importantly, 'we're on a mission of mercy to rescue my familiar, Veronica, from that awful place.'

'Really!' exclaimed Eudora. 'You've lost your familiar. Oh, you must be beside yourself with worry, you poor

116

dear wizard. I left my Slocum at home to mind the elves, but I don't know what I'd do if he ever went missing. You must let me help—and I won't take no for an answer.'

'There's really no need, Miss Pinkwhistle,' Randalf began.

'No, no, I absolutely insist!' said the witch. She reached into her capacious satchel and pulled out a tea tray with a teapot, milk jug, sugar bowl and a set of cups and saucers neatly arranged on it. 'Now, I'm sure we could all do with a nice cup of tea to settle our nerves after our little collision,' she said. 'I know I could.'

A tartan rug and a plate of shortbread appeared from the depths of the bag next, and soon everyone was sitting cross-legged in a circle sipping tea and nibbling biscuits.

'Joe?' said Ella, putting down her teacup. 'We've been talking, Edward and me.'

Now what? thought Joe, putting down his own teacup with a sigh. As if it wasn't enough that he and his big sister were stuck here in Muddle Earth, and were still no closer to getting home than when they'd first fallen through the portal, now she had fallen for Edward—and seemed determined to discuss it with him. I mean, how embarrassing was *that*?

'It's about the lamp-post,' Ella went on, taking Edward's hand and squeezing it.

'What about it?' asked Joe.

'We've made a decision,' said Edward Gorgeous, his dark eyes intense with emotion.

'When we find it,' said Ella, 'and step through the portal, Edward is coming with us.'

'There's nothing for me here in Muddle Earth,' said Edward, shaking his head. 'And now I'm no longer a thumbsucker, I want to start a new life.' He paused. 'Ella's told me all about where you come from,' he continued, his eyes growing wide. 'About traffic lights and bendy buses,' he breathed. 'And the music of the pop and the moving pictures of the tee vee. It all sounds wonderful!'

Ella smiled at Edward and gave him

a hug.

'Edward could go to college,' said Ella. 'And after that he could get a job, and then when we're older we could . . .'

'College!' spluttered Joe. 'But . . . but I saw the portrait. Of you. And your Uncle Vlad in Whatever Castle. You must be . . .' Joe hesitated. 'How old *are* you?'

'I'm the same age as Ella,' Edward replied. 'The age I was when Edwina sucked my thumb. But I'm cured now and free to live a normal life, to grow up, to fall in love . . .'

'Yes, yes,' said Joe. 'Spare me the gruesome details.' He shrugged. 'It's OK with me, but first we've got to find the lamp-post.'

'Me?' came Eudora's tinkling voice. 'I was just on my way to Goblintown, headmaster—or can I call you Randalf?'

'Headmaster will be fine,' said Randalf.

'I know a charming goblin there, Randalf,' she said, ignoring him. 'Makes all my goggle boxes for me.

119

You know, the inter-elf really has been a great success. But of course, Randalf,' she said, leaning closer and patting his arm, 'you don't need to worry. I would never dream of leaving Stinkyhogs. Not while *you're* the headmaster.'

Eudora pressed the plate of shortbread on him, which Randalf waved away.

'But that hasn't stopped me working on my little ideas,' Eudora said. 'Would you like to see my latest one?'

She reached into her black satchel and pulled out an elf that was dressed in a tight-fitting suit with a peaked cap perched on its head. It was sitting on a miniature broomstick.

'I call it the me-elf,' said Eudora proudly, 'and it's going to revolutionize the inter-elf. With these little enchanted broomsticks, the elves can travel twenty times as fast, so you can get answers to your questions twenty times as quickly.' She flapped her hands excitedly. 'And I'm going to get Grubley to make me lots and lots of tiny broomsticks, which I can enchant, because everyone who's anyone is going to want a me-elf.'

She popped it back into her satchel.

'But all that'll keep, Randalf,' she said. 'For now I shall give my undivided attention to helping you find that dear little budgie of yours.' She smiled. 'More tea?'

'No, thank you,' said Randalf weakly.

Clip-clop, clip-clop, clip-clop . . .

The sound of hoofs clomping across the marble floor echoed round the throne room of Golden Towers. A centaur in a black bow-tie and cummerbund clattered to a halt, tossed his mane and bowed to the kings and queens, who were lounging about on their velvet couches. Queen Lucy was flicking through a tattered old exercise book, the name *Lucy Pevensey-Bay—Form 2B* written on its cover in neat handwriting. King Peter and King Edmund were midway through a game of marshmallow chequers, which Edmund was losing as he couldn't resist eating his own pieces. Queen Susan, meanwhile, was having her toenails painted black by her two faun attendants.

'Your royal highnesses,' the centaur announced, 'I bring news of the lamp-post.'

'At long last,' drawled King Peter.

'About time,' yawned Queen Susan.

'Mmmppl flmmbbpl,' mumbled King Edmund.

'I agwee, Edmund, it *is* a welief,' squeaked Queen Lucy.

'I've travelled far and wide,' the centaur declared. 'I've trotted to Trollbridge, galloped to Goblintown, pranced across the Perfumed Bog and show-jumped through the Ogre Hills, but it was only when I was cantering past the Musty Mountains that I finally saw it.'

'Yes?' said King Peter.

'Spit it out,' said Queen Lucy. 'No, not you, Edmund!'

'Whatever Castle,' the centaur announced. 'It was just sitting there in the foothills, and as I approached it, I saw the lamp-post.'

'Where?' King Peter demanded.

'High up on the battlements,' the centaur replied. 'I'd have tried to catch it, but that would have meant getting inside the castle, and you know how touchy they are about visitors.'

'We'll soon see about that,' said King Peter darkly. He reached into the pocket of his velvet dressing gown and removed a shiny gold muckle, which he gave to the centaur. 'You've done very well, Fetlock.'

'Thank you, your majesty,' whinnied the centaur with a bow.

'Now, if you could just tell Big Lady Fauntleroy to gather all the little princes and princesses in the stables. I'll be with them presently,' said King Peter.

He turned on his heel and strode from the throne room and down the sweeping staircase beyond. Pausing only to pluck a flaming torch from the wall, he continued down into the very depths of the castle. There, the flickering light fell upon a studded oak

125

door with heavy hinges and a massive iron lock. Reaching inside his dressing gown, King Peter pulled out a tiny silver key and placed it in the lock.

He turned it once, twice, three times. There were three soft clicks followed by a long grinding noise, a loud grating noise, and a curious clunking sound that built up into a deafening cacophony as ancient cogs and gears and pulley-wheels slowly turned. With a gentle sigh, the studded oak door swung open on its heavy hinges and King Peter stepped inside.

The stone chamber was cavernous, with thick cobwebs curtaining its corners. In the middle of the dusty floor was a small pile of gold coins. King Peter walked over to it and bent down. He tutted softly and shook his head.

'The last of the fairy gold,' he muttered to himself as he filled the pockets of his velvet dressing gown.

He stood up, the gold muckles clinking, and stared down at the bare stone floor.

'Oh, well,' he sighed. 'It's all in a

good cause.'

He turned and left the empty treasure chamber, without bothering to lock the door behind him.

'He *bit* me!'

'Don't make a fuss, Ganymede,' said Big Lady Fauntleroy. 'You know what awful tempers they have.'

'Miss! Miss! The saddle strap won't do up. He's too fat.'

'Well, if you will keep feeding him sugar lumps, Camilla, what do you expect?' Big Lady Fauntleroy sighed. 'Do hurry up, children. King Peter will be here any minute.'

No sooner had the words left her mouth than King Peter came striding into the stables, three leather purses clutched in his hand.

The stables of Golden Towers were bright and airy, the walls whitewashed and the mosaic floor strewn with fresh sweet-smelling straw. Over each of the

nine neat wooden stalls that divided the stables hung a little board, upon which was painted a name in small decorative letters: *Candy*, *Dimples*, *Merrylegs*, *Topsy*, *Turvy*, *Tutti-Frutti*, *Tinker*, *Patches* and *Frank*.

In the stalls themselves, nine furious little unicorns with rainbow-coloured manes and tails pawed the ground and kicked out with their hoofs as the princes and princesses attempted to put saddles on their backs. Pails of water were upended, bales of hay were sent flying and saddle soap, curry combs and grooming brushes were scattered in all directions. As the last saddle was buckled and the final bridle secured—despite Candy's best efforts to bite Princess Araminta, and Merrylegs's attempts to kick Prince Rupert—King Peter stepped forward and raised his arms.

'If I could have your attention,' he drawled. 'Big Lady Fauntleroy will split you up into three groups. I shall give each group one of these,' he said, holding the leather purses up in the air. 'Now, listen carefully all of you . . .'

'That means you, too, Prince Ganymede,' said Big Lady Fauntleroy sternly.

'The future of Golden Towers depends on you.' He looked down at the row of expectant faces staring up at him. 'This is what I want you to do . . .'

Osbert the Obstinate rolled over on his bed of gravel and adjusted the boulder he used as a pillow. He pulled the coarse blanket up under his chin and tried to get comfortable. The blanket had once been a sack for mangelwurzels in Trollbridge and was grit-caked and scratchy. But it was all he had.

That, and his snuggly-wuggly, of course.

Osbert cuddled his pink cloth piglet, nuzzling up against its fraying fabric. It only had one ear, had lost half its stuffing and smelt of ogre dribble, but it felt wonderfully soft. As he stroked Pooper Pig, Osbert began to drift off to sleep . . .

'Osbert? Osbert!'

Osbert groaned and opened one of his three eyes as the dream faded away.

'What is it?' he roared.

His cave in the rolling dusty expanse of the Ogre Hills wasn't bad as far as ogre caves went. Of course, it didn't have any furniture to speak of, just a boulder for sitting on and another boulder for sitting *at*, and a third boulder for using as a pillow, or a footstool, or anything else that took your fancy. But it was quiet and secluded and an ogre could shut himself away from the hectic hustle and bustle of life in Ogre Hills, especially if he had a nice big boulder to use as a door.

Unfortunately, Osbert didn't have one of those, though he was saving up for one. In the meantime, there was nothing in his doorway but a great big hole through which anyone

131

could shout.

'There's somebody here who wants to see you,' shouted the voice.

Osbert groaned again and climbed to his feet, narrowly avoiding grazing his head on the rough ceiling of his cave as he did so. He stomped over to his doorway and, stooping down, stepped outside.

'See? What did I tell you? He's a big 'un, ain't he?'

The voice belonged to none other than Horace the Hefty, who was standing outside the cave, his hands on his hips and a broad smile on his big ogre face.

'Oh, excellent, excellent,' replied a small voice and, looking down, Osbert saw three princesses in red riding jackets. They were seated on three pretty little unicorns.

'How lovely!' Osbert exclaimed, reaching down and attempting to pet one of the unicorns on its rainbow-maned head.

With an indignant snort, the unicorn bit him on the thumb.

'Ouch!' Osbert yelped.

'You have to watch out for Candy,' said the little princess who had spoken before. 'She bites,' she added unnecessarily.

The princess reached into the purse she was clutching, pulled out a shiny gold muckle and stared up at Osbert. He was one of the biggest ogres she'd met so far in the Ogre Hills.

'You're just what we're looking for,' she said. 'How would you like to earn this lovely gold muckle?'

'Oh, please, Daddy! Pleeeeease!'

'But Guinevere, princess, I can't just drop everything because you ask me to.'

Bolgar Bloodhatchet shook his wing-helmeted head. It wouldn't do. It wouldn't do at all. First there were the battlecat trials in the Forest of Doom and straight after that the great wickerman bonfire to organize.

And as if that wasn't bad enough,

the barbarian clan of the Snarling Wolf were hosting the Barbarian Maiden Arm-Wrestling Championship this solstice—and it looked as if things could get ugly. Matilda Oxbellow had gone out of her way to insult Ethelbertha Gooseneck, saying she had hands like a Trollbridge turnip masher, and besides, black nail varnish was against the rules. Ethelbertha had told her dad and now the whole clan of the Screeching Eagle was up in arms and threatening to cause trouble at the event.

That was the trouble with barbarians. They were too hot-tempered and quick to take offence for their own good.

But what could you expect, thought Bolgar Bloodhatchet, when they were brought up in clans with names like Bellowing Bear, Charging Elk and the less fearsome, but no less argumentative, clan of the Angry Beaver?

That was why he had sent his own little bundle of joy, the apple of his eye, his darling daughter, Guinevere, away to school.

It hadn't been an easy decision, and he wasn't afraid to admit that even a big tough barbarian clan leader like himself had shed more than a couple of tears as he'd dropped his little princess off at the gates of Golden Towers school. But he knew that she would receive the finest education there in indolent lolling, divine reclining, sighing, pouting and being exquisite.

And he hadn't been disappointed. Each time she returned home for the holidays, she was even more of a little princess, poised, polite and very hard to say no to.

'Pleeeeease, Daddy,' Princess Guinevere repeated.

She had ridden into the clan's camp in Nowhere and tied the reins of her rainbow unicorn to the tent pole of her father's yak-skin yurt. Her two companions, Prince Rupert and Prince

135

Ganymede, had done the same. Never mind that Bolgar was in the middle of a very important meeting of the Custard Pie War Party; his daughter had walked straight up to his carved yak-horn throne and stamped her little foot.

'Golden Towers needs your help, Daddy,' she had said.

Bolgar Bloodhatchet had patiently explained just how busy he was. He'd told her and her two friends about the battlecat hunt, the wickerman bonfire, the barbarian maiden arm-wrestling championships, and even how complicated it was securing a good supply of custard powder at short notice. She had listened to his excuses, and then tried to get round him with that special way of hers.

'*Pleeeeeeeease*, Daddy.'

'I'm sorry, princess, but Daddy's just too busy.'

Princess Guinevere reached into the folds of her cloak and produced a purse. She held it up and shook it. The unmistakable sound of jangling gold coins filled the tent.

Princess Guinevere smiled. 'Perhaps this will change your mind,' she said sweetly.

Lionel Firebelly circled high over the Here-Be-Dragon Mountains. With powerful beats of his deep crimson wings, Lionel sought out strong updraughts of air as he steered a zigzag course across the sky with swishes of his emerald-tipped tail. The sunlight played on the rich bottle-green scales of his back and on his burnished copper underbelly. The jagged ridge of bony plates that ran down his back from the top of his head to the tip of his tail stood out ruby-red against the bright blue of the sky.

Swooping down in order to take advantage of the glassy surface of a mountain lake, Lionel admired his reflection. The magnificent wings, the iridescent scales, the wonderfully sinuous tail . . . and all so thrillingly, eye-catchingly bright and colourful!

What a magnificent specimen of a dragon he was, thought Lionel, doing a triple back-loop followed by another swooping fly-past to catch his reflection in the lake once more.

Soaring back high into the sky, he exhaled a great jet of flame from his nostrils in pure joy at his own splendour.

138

Surely no other dragon could possibly complete with Lionel Firebelly when it came to sheer good looks, he thought to himself proudly.

Not that he'd ever dream of allowing them to try. That was why he liked to keep himself to himself and not have anything to do with those other dragons with their gaudy wings and overpolished scales.

They were all such show-offs, thought Lionel primly, or at least they would be if they ever got together— which they almost never did because, like Lionel, most dragons kept themselves to themselves.

He flew on, careful to make sure that he kept a good distance between himself and the other dragons circling the skies over the Here-Be-Dragon Mountains. Just as he was about to head back towards his comfortable cave, with its admittedly small but pleasingly glittery hoard of treasure, Lionel spotted something far below.

It was bright and shiny and glinted enticingly in the sunlight. Folding his crimson wings and arching his emerald-tipped tail, Lionel dived down towards the tempting object. Moments later, he landed on the boulder-strewn valley floor below.

There, sitting on a rock, was a gold muckle.

Lionel let out a little cry of delight together with a couple of perfectly formed smoke rings and reached for the coin—only for it to be snatched away by a small pampered hand.

'Not so fast,' came a haughty childlike voice.

Lionel looked up. Three little princes, each of them dressed in red riding cloaks and clutching the bridle of their own rainbow unicorn, stood in a line staring back at him.

Prince Caspian held the coin between a thumb and forefinger.

'If you want this gold muckle,' he said, 'you'll have to earn it.'

Golden Towers Finishing School for

Little Princes and Princesses was a hive of activity. The battlements were thronged with barbarians in winged helmets and tooled-leather breastplates, busy unpacking yak-skin backpacks and unrolling fleecy sleeping bags. Swords, shields, battleaxes and large sacks marked *Custard Powder* littered the stone walkways and clogged the battlement steps.

'By the whiskers of Freya the Beardy!' roared their leader, a huge barbarian with a curling black beard. 'Get the saucepans on the fire. And don't let the milk boil over!'

In the courtyard below, seven enormous ogres were sitting around the beautiful marble fountain, soaking their enormous feet and nuzzling their snuggly-wugglies.

'Whoops!' said an ogre as he accidentally knocked the head off the marble statue of a water nymph riding a dolphin. 'Silly me!'

He picked up his pink fabric pig and rubbed it against his stubbly cheek.

'You're much more cuddly than that marble mermaid, Pooper,' he said.

High above the courtyard, perched on each of the four golden towers of the castle, were four dragons eyeing each other critically. The crimson-winged dragon with the bottle-green scales and emerald tip to his tail on the north tower snorted scornfully and stuck his nose in the air. On the south tower, a dappled mauve and pink dragon with distinctive striped wings pretended not to notice as she filed her talons with a lump of pumice-stone. Meanwhile, the dragons on the east and west towers were engaged in a staring contest to see which of them would blink first. The east-tower dragon spread her magnificent yellow wings for maximum effect, while the west-tower dragon puffed out his gaudy turquoise chest in response.

'Hmm, you're looking good, Lionel,' said the dragon on the north tower to himself.

'Nobody's got wings like yours,' the east-tower dragon told herself.

'This tail's to die for,' the west-tower dragon congratulated himself.

'Rise above it . . . Rise above it all, Cynthia,' murmured the dragon on the south tower.

Over the main gate was a covered balcony that jutted out from the castle wall. The little princes and princesses were seated along it on small cushioned stools with seat belts. Big Lady Fauntleroy sat behind them in what looked like a barber's chair, while in front were four padded thrones in which sat the kings and queens of Golden Towers, strapped securely into place. King Peter looked down from the balcony at the ornamental gardens and landscaped grounds stretching out before them, then turned to the others.

'Ready?' he asked.

Queen Susan nodded.

King Edmund grunted.

Queen Lucy smiled thinly. 'Weady,' she said.

King Peter turned back and reached

143

for the heavy iron lever that was bolted next to the brass steering wheel in front of him. He seized the lever and shoved it firmly forward.

There was a *rumble* and a *clang* and a resounding *clunk!* and the whole castle began to shake.

'Can't see them anywhere,' sighed Eraguff, flapping his beige wings as he hovered unsteadily above the rolling grasslands north of the Musty Mountains.

'Nor can I,' admitted Joe.

To his right, the stair-carpet fluttered in mid-air, Randalf, Norbert, Edward and Ella all scanning the ground below. To his left, Eudora Pinkwhistle was perched on her broomstick, Dyson, and doing the same. The aerial collision had knocked them badly off course and they had lost the trail of footprints they'd been following.

'Hang on a minute. What's that?' Eudora's voice rang out. She pointed. 'Over there!'

A little way off, heading away across the prairie, were the smudgy imprints of a pair of giant mechanical feet.

'Footprints!' exclaimed Eraguff and Joe together.

'Well done, Eudora,' said Randalf, suppressing a yawn. 'Now, let's try not to lose sight of them again,' he said, settling back down on his carpet step. His head began to nod.

They set off on the trail of the footprints, which headed in the direction of the mountain range on the horizon. They flew on through the late afternoon and some time later, as the sun was sinking low in the sky, found themselves in the stale canyons and stuffy valleys of the Musty Mountains. As they rounded a tall pointy peak, Eudora let out a little squeak.

'The castle!' she cried out. 'We've found it.'

There, stepping daintily over a ravine, was a beautiful building of white stone with elegant carved battlements, a shady courtyard and four golden towers at its corners around which were coiled sleeping

146

dragons. Powered by a vast invisible engine that shuddered and thrummed in the very depths of the castle, its two great mechanical legs of shiny, oiled brass wheezed and hissed as they strode on through the mountains.

'Oh, no,' groaned Joe as he stared in disbelief. 'That's not Whatever. We've been following the wrong castle!'

'It's Golden Towers!' exclaimed Edward, sitting up on the flying carpet, 'or as I once knew it, when it belonged to my Aunt Heidi, Whoever Castle.' His eyes misted over. 'But that was all so long ago.'

Eudora looked at him quizzically from her broomstick, then reached into her satchel and drew out the me-elf. Holding it up to her mouth, she whispered into the elf's ear before throwing it into the air. The me-elf hovered for an instant above her head, then whizzed off on its tiny broomstick and disappeared into the distance.

Far ahead, the castle of Golden Towers descended the mountainside and began marching across the broad plain on the other side of the Musty

Mountains. Joe, Eraguff, Eudora and the flying stair-carpet followed. Out over the plain, it soon became clear that the castle was following footprints of its own, and before long a second castle came into view. It was sitting motionless in the middle of the dusty plain, the great disc of the Enchanted Lake shimmering in the distance behind it.

'Whatever!' Joe shouted from Eraguff's back.

On the stair-carpet, Randalf woke up with a start, while Norbert stared, his triple eyes wide with surprise.

'*Two* castles?' he said and scratched his head.

Just then there came a whistling, whizzing sound as the me-elf on the tiny broomstick came hurtling back and landed on Eudora's outstretched arm.

'Goggle! Goggle! Goggle!' it trilled. 'Whoever Castle was built by Count Vlad the Tickler for his wife, Heidi the Gorgeous, when she had finally had enough of being tickled and chased with a feather-duster. Furthermore, Countess Heidi decided to turn

Whoever Castle into a refuge for any over-tickled denizens of Muddle Earth, *whoever* they might be.'

The me-elf paused for breath, adjusted its cap, then continued.

'Just like Whatever Castle, Whoever Castle was built with the treasure trove that Count Vlad had dug up, creating a hole now known as the Sandpit. Originally, the towers of both castles were tiled with slate quarried from the banks of the Enchanted River. Dust settling on these magic rooftops at dusk and dawn became the legendary sunset and sunrise dust. After falling into disrepair, in recent times the empty castle of Whoever was taken over by the self-appointed kings and queens of Muddle Earth, who replaced the slate tiles with burnished gold when they turned the castle into the Golden Towers Finishing School for Little Princes and Princesses . . .'

'Thank you, that was fascinating,' said Eudora enthusiastically as she stared at the two castles ahead. Golden Towers had stopped in front of Whatever Castle and was now in the process of sitting itself down. Eudora shoved the me-elf back into her satchel, its head disappearing inside with a little squeak. 'I wonder what *they're* up to?' she murmured, bringing her broomstick to a hover.

'I don't know,' said Joe, as Eraguff slowed down beside her, 'but I have the feeling we're about to find out.'

'Oh dear,' said Randalf from the top of the stair-carpet. 'I do hope there isn't going to be any unpleasantness.

For Veronica's sake . . .'

At that moment, a loudhailer emerged from the covered balcony above the main gate of Golden Towers. A voice rang out.

'Professors of Whatever! We are the Kings and Queens of Golden Towers, and we believe that you are harbouring an escaped lamp-post. We demand that you let us in to claim it!'

'My apologies,' came a loud but polite voice in response, 'but we do our best to discourage visitors here at the university. So, if you wouldn't mind turning round and going away, we'd be awfully grateful.'

'Well, if that's the way you want to play it,' said King Peter hotly, 'then you leave us with no choice . . .'

'Oh, howwid old teachers like you make me so cwoss!' added Queen Lucy crossly.

'I'm sorry you feel that way,' came Lord Asbow's voice from the battlements of Whatever, 'but I'll have to leave matters up to the castle now. It's fully automated to repel invaders.'

As Joe watched, there came a loud

whumph, then another, and another, and another, in rapid succession, as four plump vacuum-cleaner bags shot out of a row of nozzles set into the rotating top of the castle's central tower. They sailed up, high over the battlements of Whatever Castle, before coming hurtling down towards the gleaming rooftops of Golden Towers.

'Sunset dust!' bellowed King Peter.

'Dwagons, attack!' commanded Queen Lucy.

From the four corners of the castle came deep throaty roars as the four dragons uncoiled themselves and sprang into action.

The crimson-winged dragon with the bottle-green scales launched himself from the roof of the north tower and, lunging to his right, caught the first plump vacuum-cleaner bag that was tumbling down out of the sky. At the same time, the mauve and pink dragon with the striped wings dived down from the south tower and plucked a second vacuum-cleaner bag out of the air, inches above the cobblestones of the courtyard below. Spreading her wings,

152

she soared up into the air.

Meanwhile, spiralling down from the east tower like a streak of summer lightning, the yellow-winged dragon scooped up the third bag in both arms and hugged it to her chest.

The fourth dragon, in the meantime, had executed an elegant triple back-loop and lassoed the incoming fourth vacuum-cleaner bag in the coils of his tail, and was spinning round to circle the golden spire of the west tower. He puffed out his turquoise chest with pride.

'Bwavo!' Queen Lucy exclaimed.

High above the castle, the dragons hovered for a moment, their gaudy wings lit up by the evening sun. One after another, they tossed their vacuum-cleaner bags up above their heads. Then, opening their jaws wide, the dragons sent jets of flame billowing after them.

The next moment, the darkening sky was lit up by a series of spectacular explosions as the fire engulfed each vacuum-cleaner bag in turn. Showers of pink and gold and blue sparks crackled and fizzed.

'Oooooh . . . Aaaaaaahhhh!' came voices from the courtyard and turrets of Golden Towers.

On the battlements opposite, the professors of the University of Whatever looked at each other in dismay.

'Oh dear,' said Lord Asbow. 'Perhaps we should try that again.'

From the covered balcony of Golden

Towers, Queen Lucy's voice rang out. 'Barbawians, attack!'

A hundred wing-helmeted heads popped up above the walls of the castle and the air filled with raucous battle oaths.

'Mighty Wotulf, make my flan fly true!'

'Curdle not my custard, Freya of the Flaxen Beard!'

'By the tinkling of your pixie boots, little Olaf, guide my pie!'

Bolgar Bloodhatchet drew himself up to his full height and raised a fist above his head. In response, the massed clans of the Custard Pie War Party leaped to their feet.

The clan of the Screeching Eagle balanced the broad discs of their *tartes de crème* in the palms of their hands, while the clan of the Bellowing Bear gripped the crenellated edges of their whipped vanilla pies in trembling fingers. Beside them, the clan of the Charging Elk and the clan of the Snarling Wolf cradled their custard flans and steaming sweet quiches in the crooks of their muscle-bound arms as the clan of the Angry Beaver wiped away crumbs from the corners of their mouths and tried to hide the nibbled corners of their custard turnovers.

'Fire!' bellowed Bolgar Bloodhatchet and dropped his fist.

A hundred custard pies flew through the air towards Whatever Castle. They whistled over the heads of the cowering professors on the battlements and splattered against the central tower, clogging the row of nozzles at its rotating top as they did so. The tower stopped rotating and the vacuum-cleaner bags that were about to shoot out of its nozzles exploded within its ivory walls with muffled *whumphs*.

The tower shuddered, and from deep within, there came the sound of grinding gears and clashing cogwheels. The tower rattled and shook. Then, after a series of stifled bangs and crashes, it abruptly fell still.

'I say!' exclaimed Lord Asbow, his outraged voice mingling with the howls of his Labrador. 'That wasn't very

sporting! But throw as many custard pies as you like, you're still not coming in!'

'Pwepare the battewing wam!' Queen Lucy gave the command.

In the courtyard, the biggest of the seven ogres put his pink fabric pig in his pocket and lay on the ground. Stooping down, the other ogres—three on one side, three on the other—gently picked him up and tucked him securely under their massive arms. As the gates of Golden Towers swung open, the ogres stomped through them carrying their companion head first. Gathering speed, their huge feet throwing up clods of earth, the ogres thundered towards the raised drawbridge of Whatever Castle.

'*OOOF!*' grunted the ogre battering ram, to the accompaniment of splintering wood and breaking hinges, as his huge head smashed into the door.

'*OOOF! OOOF! OOOF!*' the battering ram exclaimed as his companions swung him repeatedly at the disintegrating timbers.

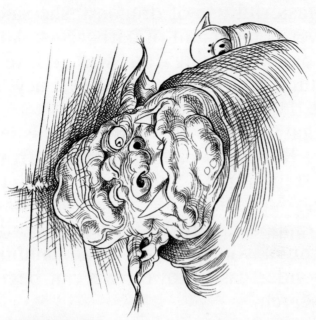

CRASH!!

The drawbridge collapsed and, dropping the battering ram, the other six ogres stormed into the castle.

'You're much more cuddly than that wooden drawbridge, Pooper,' the ogre battering ram muttered as he pulled his snuggly-wuggly from his pocket and followed the others inside.

From his vantage point on Eraguff's back, Joe had watched as the siege of Whatever Castle had unfolded. He had never seen anything like it. Hovering by his side, Eudora had shared his fascination.

'Masterful use of dragons,' she said. 'Clever deployment of barbarians. And the ogre battering ram was a lovely finishing touch. That Queen Lucy is quite the little general!'

'That's as may be, Miss Pinkwhistle,' said Randalf, calling across from the stair-carpet, 'but we're here to rescue Veronica.' He raised his staff and tapped lightly. 'O carpet of aerial delight, if you wouldn't mind landing on yonder castle tower, we can begin our search.'

'Certainly, O great magician,' the stair-carpet whispered, shaking its tassels and speeding off towards Whatever Castle, the witch following close behind on her broomstick.

'Randalf! Eudora! *Wait!*' cried Joe. 'Watch out for the sunset dust!'

But they didn't hear him. The stair-carpet swooped down on to the top of a tall tower at the back of the castle and landed in a cloud of dust. Eudora and Dyson landed next to it.

'Ella! Edward! Cover your mouths!' called Joe as first Randalf, then Norbert fell fast asleep and slumped

160

from their steps on the carpet. 'We're coming to get you!'

Eager to please, Eraguff beat his wings and raced forward, just in time to scoop Joe's sister and her boyfriend from the dusty carpet, itself now gently snoring. Looking back over his shoulder, Joe saw Eudora crumple beside Randalf, her snoozing broom in her arms.

'Over there,' Joe said, pointing to the battlements, now empty of professors, who were streaming down the steps that led to the courtyard.

Eraguff landed gently and set Edward and Ella on the ground. Joe jumped from his back.

'You're getting better and better at this, Eraguff,' he complimented his friend, patting him on the neck. He turned to the other two. 'It's OK,' he said. 'You can breathe now.'

But Edward wasn't listening. He was staring at the gleaming ivory towers, a haunted look in his eyes.

'This place,' he murmured. 'It brings it all back to me. It was on these very battlements that Edwina Lovely tricked me into letting her suck my thumb.' He shuddered.

'Oh, Edward,' said Ella. 'That was the past. It's the future we must think of.' She turned to Joe. 'We've got to find that portal . . .'

Just then, from far below in the courtyard, came a shrill voice. 'Stand back, wiff-waff! And make way for my big bwother, King Peter!'

Joe peered down to see the kings and queens of Golden Towers step through the castle gate. They strode into the cobbled courtyard, where the crestfallen professors of the university awaited them, their pets fluttering, fidgeting and breaking wind around them. King Edmund and Queen Susan were carrying a large net between them. Queen Lucy had a lasso coiled over her shoulder, while King Peter was holding a sack of cement in one hand and a sturdy catapult in the other.

'We've come for the lamp-post,' he said. 'And we're not leaving without it.' He brandished his catapult. 'I'm going to smash its light bulb,' he said fiercely. 'And set its feet in concrete in the basement of Golden Towers,' he added, flourishing the sack of cement. 'That way, the portal will be locked away where it can't do any harm!'

'And we shall never have to weturn to that howwid school ever again!' Queen Lucy added with a stamp of her foot.

Lord Asbow stared back at King Peter unhappily. 'This really isn't the way we do things here at the university,' he protested. 'I'm afraid you're going to have to pay for a new drawbridge. And Muddle Earth only knows how much it'll cost to repair the dust-catapult . . .'

'Peter. It's over there,' hissed Queen Lucy urgently and pointed to the far corner of the courtyard.

All eyes turned in the direction of her pointing finger. And there, in the shadows cast by the stone steps that led up to the battlements, sat the little lamp-post, its wrought iron legs neatly crossed one over the other and its light bulb dimmed.

Lord Asbow shrugged. 'If it means you'll go away and leave us in peace, then take the confounded thing,' he said, 'though in my opinion, you have the most appalling manners for royalty.'

The kings and queens ignored him. With the net raised, Queen Susan and King Edmund tiptoed towards the lamp-post from one side, while King Peter put down the sack of cement and approached from the other side, his catapult raised and loaded. Queen Lucy crept stealthily behind him, uncoiling the lasso as she went.

From the battlements above, Joe, Ella and Edward looked on helplessly. Joe shook his head. If the kings and queens destroyed the lamp-post, he and his big sister would never get home. Behind them, Eraguff's ears twitched.

'What's that?' the dragon whispered.

Joe stared. In the shadows to the left of the sleeping lamp-post, he thought he detected the slightest of shimmers in the air, like a net curtain twitching in a summer breeze. And the faintest of smells—a mixture of boiled cabbage and floor polish. And a sound, so soft Joe might almost have been imagining it—the sound of distant voices in a classroom somewhere chanting their nine-times table.

'It's the portal!' Joe exclaimed, then frowned. 'Though it doesn't sound or smell like it leads to our house . . .'

King Edmund, Queen Susan and Queen Lucy crept as close to the lamp-post as they dared, net and lasso at the ready, before pausing and looking over to their older brother for a sign. King Peter raised the catapult, closed one eye and took aim at the lamp-post's light bulb.

Suddenly, the lamp-post burst into dazzling light.

'Oh!' gasped King Peter, dropping the catapult and shielding his eyes.

'Oh!' gasped Queen Lucy, blinded for an instant and tripping over King Edmund's pudgy foot.

'Oh!' gasped Queen Susan. The lamp-post leaped up and whisked the net out of her hands and encircled the four of them.

'Mppllffwb!' protested King Edmund indignantly as the net tightened and he was squashed up against his brother and sisters.

Joe watched the lamp-post hook the bulging net with one foot and twirl it around. Then, with a low chuckle, it kicked out and released one end, sending the kings and queens tumbling into the shadows. Like four pebbles dropping into a pool, Peter, Edmund, Susan and Lucy created ripples in the air as they fell into the portal and disappeared from view.

With its light bulb glowing brightly, the lamp-post gave a little hop, skip and jump before sprinting off across

the courtyard, over the broken drawbridge and out of the castle.

'Oh, no!' wailed Ella.

'It's getting away!' cried Edward.

'Not again,' moaned Joe.

Eraguff leaped up and took to the air. 'Don't worry,' he called back eagerly. 'I'll catch it.'

Before Joe could say anything, the dragon had flapped over the castle walls and was gone.

From the top of the tower above him, Joe could hear a chorus of snoring as Randalf, Norbert and Eudora slept on, oblivious to all the excitement. Meanwhile, down below in the courtyard, Lord Asbow and the professors watched the bemused ogres shuffle apologetically out of the castle.

'Sorry about all the mess,' said Osbert the Obstinate. 'Lovely soft Labrador, by the way,' he called as he put back the shattered boards of the drawbridge behind him as best he could.

Moments later, one by one, the propped-up timbers of the drawbridge fell down again as the earth began to tremble.

STOMP! STOMP! STOMP! STOMP!

The towers swayed. The glass rattled in the windows. And pastry crumbs danced on the cobblestones of the courtyard as it shook.

Lord Asbow sighed heavily and rolled his eyes. 'Now what?'

'They did *what*?' Big Lady Fauntleroy gasped, her three chins wobbling.

'They just disappeared. All four of them,' Osbert the Obstinate repeated. He scratched his head. 'One moment they were there, the next moment they were gone.'

'Gone,' Big Lady Fauntleroy echoed in a shocked voice. She sat down heavily on one of the empty thrones that stood on the balcony and grabbed the large brass steering wheel for support. 'They must have fallen through the portal. Of course, that was always the danger. I warned them, but their minds were made up.' She shook her head sadly, then looked around, suddenly aware that all eyes were on her. The little princes and princesses perched on their padded stools at the back of the balcony, their lower lips trembling. The seven ogres, the largest one with a purple bruise beginning to form on the top of his head, stood in a cluster by the door. Above them, lining the battlements, a hundred barbarians in winged helmets looked down on the balcony, their faces grim and questioning. On the four towers perched the four gaudily coloured dragons, impatiently blowing smoke rings as they watched Big Lady Fauntleroy through narrowed yellow eyes.

'And now they're gone.' She shrugged her large shoulders. 'So I suppose that's the end of that.'

Her plump fingers drummed on the brass steering wheel as a thought came into her head. With the kings and queens no longer there, Golden Towers Finishing School for Little Princes and Princesses would need new leadership.

'But Big Lady Fauntleroy,' said one of the little princes, 'what are we going to *do*?'

Big Lady Fauntleroy's eyes sparkled and her chins wobbled. 'That's *Headmistress* Fauntleroy to you, Prince Adrian,' she announced proudly.

STOMP! STOMP! STOMP! STOMP!

Startled plumes of flame shot from the open mouths of the dragons, while a low murmur spread through the ranks of the barbarians on the battlements. Down on the balcony, the ogres' triple eyes bulged with astonishment, and the little princes and princesses almost fell off their stools in surprise. On the padded throne, Headmistress Fauntleroy gripped the brass steering wheel and stared.

Advancing towards them across the rolling plain was what appeared to be a forest. Except this forest had feet— big gnarled rooty feet, one hundred and twenty-eight of them, pounding on the plain as they approached the two castles.

STOMP! STOMP! STOMP! STOMP!

As the forest drew near, the individual trees could be seen more clearly. They were huge. Towering chestnuts, mighty oaks, rough-barked pines and swaying willows. Bright twinkling eyes stared out from knot-holes, and bark-fringed mouths gaped open.

'We ain't beeches or birches or blackthorn, we ain't maple or poplar or lime; we ain't ashes or aspens, we ain't elms, we ain't oaks, we ain't chestnut or walnut or pine!' sang the Giggle Glade Mob, the Babbling Brook Boys, the Dingly Dell Gang and the Wild Wood Crew in unison.

'We're aints! We're aints! We're aints!'
STOMP! STOMP! STOMP! STOMP!

On the balcony of Golden Towers, Headmistress Fauntleroy grew pale.

'I think it's time we were on our way,' she said.

On the towers, the four dragons nodded. On the battlements, the barbarians quickly agreed, while the ogres clattered down the steps from the balcony to the courtyard and attempted to hide behind the marble fountain.

'Singing trees,' gasped Osbert the Obstinate, hugging his pink fabric pig tightly to his huge chest. 'Scary!'

The headmistress grabbed the iron lever beside the steering wheel and pushed it forward, while the little princes and princesses tightened the straps on their padded stools. With a hissing of pistons and a  grinding of gears, Golden Towers rose up on its mechanical legs and began trotting off across the plains.

In the branches of the mighty oak-like aint who was striding out in front, four flower fairies peered through the leaves.

'Let it go,' Pesticide commanded. She pointed to Whatever Castle. *'That's* the one we want!'

From the battlements of Whatever Castle, Joe, Ella and Edward looked on in horrified fascination as what appeared to be huge walking trees burst into the courtyard below. The professors seemed equally dumbstruck as the trees surrounded them. Hugging their pets and gazing up at the gnarled, knotty faces leering down at them, they whimpered softly.

Clutching his Labrador around its ample belly, Lord Asbow found his voice. 'Oh dear, not *more* visitors,' he moaned.

'Come on, you two,' Joe whispered urgently as he dashed off along the battlements towards the nearest tower.

But before Ella and Edward could follow, they were grasped by the willowy arms of one of the Babbling Brook Boys who had crept up the steps to the battlements.

'Put me down! Put me down!' protested Ella, struggling as the willow passed her to his companions below.

Seconds later, the pair of them found themselves on the cobbles of the courtyard beside the trembling professors and their pets, surrounded by trees.

'Do I know you?' Lord Asbow asked, distracted for a moment from his and his fellow professors' predicament. 'You're not Stibbing and Chate from the Blueprints and Pie Charts Department by any chance?'

Before Ella or Edward could answer, an imperious voice sounded from the branches of the tall oak towering over them.

'Professors of the University of Whatever, your castle is ours!'

The four flower fairies burst from the foliage and fluttered down to land on the cobblestones below.

'The jeer-leaders!' Edward gasped.

'But you've got wings!' exclaimed Ella.

'No speaking unless you're spoken to!' boomed the towering oak. 'Stand up straight and stop that shuffling!' he added bossily.

'Thank you, Bert Shiverwithers,' said Pesticide, tossing back her green hair and folding her arms. She eyed Edward and Ella dismissively. 'Oh, if it isn't the broomball captain and his barbarian girlfriend,' she sneered. 'Shouldn't you be in some stupid class or other back at Stinkyhogs?'

Lord Asbow gave Ella and Edward a quizzical look.

Pesticide turned away. 'Still, who cares?' she said, pacing backwards and forwards in front of the professors. 'I've got far more important things on my mind, such as the lamp-post . . .'

'Not you as well,' groaned Lord Asbow.

Pesticide ignored him. 'We have to find the lamp-post because we wish to enter the portal. The two objects already in our possession will guide us

to the third. We need to retrieve the flat-pack wardrobe you professors so carelessly allowed to fall into it.'

'That was Mr Fluffy's fault,' Lord Asbow muttered.

'For included in that flat-pack,' Pesticide continued, 'was a seemingly insignificant tool for tightening screws. Flat, made of metal and shaped like an acorn. You professors had no idea of its true value, unlike we flower fairies.'

Ella frowned and reached into the pocket of her black cut-off jeans.

'Because, rather than a simple screwdriver,' Pesticide went on, 'that tool was none other than the fabled third object of the old old fairy magic . . .' She paused for dramatic effect. 'The Acorn of Abundance!'

'Well, if you're looking for the lamp-post,' said Lord Asbow loftily, 'I'm afraid you're out of luck. It ran off just before you arrived.'

'Out of luck?' said Nettle.

'Ran off?' said Thistle.

'*Just* before we arrived?' groaned Briar-Rose.

'Then we must follow it!' Pesticide

cried, flapping her wings and hovering just above the cobblestones. 'Which way did it go?'

'Not a clue, I'm afraid,' said Lord Asbow airily as an appalling smell rose up from the black Labrador in his arms. 'Tricky fellows, lamp-posts. It could be absolutely anywhere by now.'

Pesticide clenched her mittened hands in frustration. 'If I can't find the portal,' she screamed, 'then how on Muddle Earth am I ever going to get my hands on the Acorn of Abundance?'

'This acorn you're wailing about,' said Ella, taking a step forward and pulling her hand from her pocket. 'Does it look anything like this?'

She opened her fist and there, resting in her palm, was the curious little tool she'd used to tighten the screws on the doors of the flat-pack wardrobe.

'The Acorn of Abundance!' exclaimed Pesticide, snatching it from Ella. She paused and looked up. 'But how did *you* get hold of this?'

'Well,' Ella began, 'I was—'

'Oh, who cares?' said Pesticide, turning delightedly to the other flower fairies. 'The important thing is, it's ours now—and we won't have to go chasing after that stupid lamp-post after all!'

Her gossamer wings were a blur of movement as she flitted around the courtyard excitedly.

'Nettle, Thistle, the Plant Pot of Power!' she commanded. 'Briar-Rose, the Trowel of Destiny!' She hovered in front of the oak-like leader of the aints. 'And Bert Shiverwithers, move everyone well back. You need plenty of space for old old fairy magic . . .'

179

Joe hadn't looked back as he'd run the length of the battlements and leaped through the open window of the nearest tower. He'd crouched down in the shadows inside and waited for Ella and Edward to join him, only to hear their shouts of protest as the weeping willow had carried them off.

What now? he wondered with a sinking feeling in the pit of his stomach. First Randalf, Norbert and Eudora had fallen victim to the sunset dust, and now Ella and Edward had been caught by a walking tree. And as for the lamp-post, they were still no nearer to finding it than when they'd started!

'Joe? Joe, is that you?' came a voice.

Joe looked around. He was standing in a familiar-looking workshop full of odd woodworking tools.

'Experimental woodwork,' he muttered. His gaze fell upon a small birdcage hanging from the ceiling. 'Veronica!' Joe exclaimed, rushing over and opening the door to the cage. 'What happened to you?'

Veronica hopped out on to his

shoulder. 'You may well ask,' she said with feeling. 'When you fell off the castle tower, Joe, I tried to follow you, but a gust of wind blew me through a window, and I ended up in this preposterous excuse for a workshop. One of those crazy professors locked me up in that cage. He was convinced I was your pet and was determined to look after me until you returned. Wouldn't take no for an answer. I mean, me—a *pet*!' she chirped indignantly. 'Have you ever heard of such a thing?'

'It's good to have you back,' said Joe. 'But we're in big trouble . . .'

'That doesn't surprise me where Randalf's concerned,' said Veronica. 'What's he done now?'

'Well . . .' Joe began.

'Who's there?' came a rather timid-sounding voice, and a dishevelled, bespectacled figure stepped out of the

shadows in the far corner of the workshop. He was holding a small golden hamster in his hands.

'Mr Fluffy?' said Joe. 'It *is* Mr Fluffy, isn't it?'

'Joe the Barbarian,' said Mr Fluffy. 'Weren't you off with the headmaster searching for the Goblet of Porridge? Did you have any luck?'

'No,' admitted Joe, 'not much.' He frowned. 'You used to work here, didn't you? You made that wardrobe, the flat-pack one . . .'

'Oh, the *Tumnus*! That was my best work!' Mr Fluffy exclaimed, his beady eyes twinkling. His face fell. 'Until it fell into that portal. Unfortunate business,' he admitted. He gripped his hamster tightly. 'And they punished me for it. Lord Asbow and the others. But it's all right now, isn't it, Daemian? Those nasty old professors couldn't keep us apart forever, could they, boy?'

Mr Fluffy kissed the hamster tenderly on the head, his beady eyes misting with tears behind his wire-framed spectacles. He looked up at Joe and cleared his throat.

'I saw the castle walk past Stinkyhogs, and despite my disgrace, I just couldn't help myself. I knew I had to follow it if I was ever to be reunited with my Daemian.' He smiled. 'I sneaked in over the battlements while the castle was distracted by Golden Towers. And here I am.'

Just then, two branch-like arms burst through the open window of the workshop and weeping-willow fingers seized Mr Fluffy and Joe.

'Get off!' shouted Joe. 'Leave me alone!'

'It's all right, Daemian, I'll protect you,' wailed Mr Fluffy, pushing the little hamster into the top pocket of his tweed jacket.

'Resistance is futile,' came a bossy voice as the arms dragged Joe and Mr Fluffy across the workshop and out through the window.

Veronica flapped after them.

On the battlements outside, the enormous aint tucked Joe and Mr Fluffy securely under his arms, before turning on his root-like feet and descending the stone steps to the courtyard below. There it unceremoniously dumped the two of them on to the cobblestones next to a group of bewildered-looking professors and their pets.

'Found two more,' the aint informed Bert Shiverwithers. 'They were hiding in this torture chamber. Horrible, it was. Sawdust and wood-shavings all over the place,' he added with a leafy shudder.

'Joe, are you all right?' said Ella, as she and Edward helped him to his feet.

'No talking!' barked Bert Shiverwithers.

Joe straightened his robes. Veronica fluttered down and landed on his shoulder. Behind Joe, Lord Asbow leaned forward.

'Caught you in your workshop, eh, Jefferson?' he whispered. 'Bad luck.'

Joe smiled weakly. He looked around. The courtyard was full of the towering tree-like creatures, their knobbly knot-hole eyes all fixed on the four flower fairies with the interesting hairstyles standing at its centre. The one with green hair and a severe fringe seemed to be in charge.

'Nettle, Thistle. Put the Plant Pot of Power down there,' she instructed.

The two flower fairies—one with straggly braids of bleached white and the other with a shock of purple spikes—put the small battered-looking cup down on the cobbles.

Joe gasped. 'The Goblet of Porridge,' he breathed.

'Briar-Rose, the Trowel of Destiny,' said Pesticide.

The flower fairy with the magenta bob placed a silver object with a gold handle in Pesticide's mittened hand.

Joe's eyes widened. 'The Sword in the Scone,' he breathed.

Pesticide held up her other hand. Grasped in her mittened fingers was a flat metal disc. 'The Acorn of Abundance!' she proclaimed.

Joe gave a puzzled frown. 'The thing for tightening the screws in the flat-pack wardrobe?' he breathed.

In the centre of the courtyard, Pesticide crouched down in front of the plant pot and leaned forward. Carefully, she placed the acorn in the bowl of the pot. Then, with trembling fingers, she inserted the silver blade of the trowel into a narrow slit at the base of the pot and turned its gold handle. As she did so, there was a metallic *clink* and the acorn dropped down inside the stem of the pot, like a coin in a slot-machine.

'And all without instructions,' said Lord Asbow, impressed.

'Shhh!' hissed Bert Shiverwithers.

Pesticide straightened up and stepped back, her gossamer wings fluttering excitedly as the Plant Pot of Power began to tremble and shake. Suddenly, from deep within, a beam of silver light shot up into the air, followed by another and another and another, until the whole plant pot was glowing like a bright star.

Shielding his eyes and peering into the light, Joe could just make out silvery tendrils snaking their way over the rim of the plant pot and coiling down the sides. They grew thicker and more tangled as they enveloped the pot and the trowel, and spread out across the cobbles like the roots of a tree.

Larger strands erupted from the centre of the pot and, plaiting themselves together, rose up into the air to form a shining silver trunk. Branches appeared, dividing and subdividing, and subdividing again, until Joe found himself staring at a tall glowing tree covered with rustling silver-foil leaves.

Around him, the professors gave out small gasps of disbelief and grasped their pets protectively.

'Old old fairy magic,' said Lord Asbow thoughtfully as yet another appalling smell rose up from his Labrador. 'Powerful stuff.'

Tiny gold buds sprouted at the tips of every branch and grew steadily in size until the entire tree was laden with clinking clusters of gold coins. Pesticide gave a little whoop of joy. She reached out a mittened glove and shook the silver trunk of the tree. With a metallic clatter, coins rained down on to the cobblestones to form a carpet of gold beneath the tree. In the branches above, more gold muckles sprouted to take their place.

'Rich! Rich!' Pesticide cackled, linking arms with Nettle, Thistle and Briar-Rose, and dancing round the fabled muckle tree of fairy legend. 'Rich beyond our wildest dreams!'

'We can buy anything!' laughed Briar-Rose. 'Black nail varnish by the barrelful . . .'

'And all the stripy black-and-white

tights and big boots we could ever want!' chortled Nettle.

'We can be waited on hand and wing,' nodded Thistle. 'And never have to do what our silly old parents tell us ever again!'

'That's just the start,' said Pesticide darkly. 'Now that we're rich, with our friends the aints and this castle at our command, we can throw out those stupid wizards and rule Muddle Earth ourselves!'

'At *your* command, did you say?' said Lord Asbow, putting down his Labrador and stepping forward. 'I'm afraid, my young fairy, the instructions for operating the castle are extremely complicated and take years of careful study to master. I think you'll find that, when it comes to Whatever Castle,' he said grandly, '*I* am in command.'

'Then I command you to make it do what I want,' said Pesticide, stamping her foot.

'Out of the question,' said Lord Asbow firmly and folded his arms. 'And neither you, your gold muckles nor your big forest friends here can change my mind.'

'We'll see about that,' said Pesticide menacingly. 'Aints, seize them!'

The aints shot out branch-like arms and wrapped them round the terrified professors and their pets, pinning them to the spot. Joe, Ella and Edward found themselves in the clutches of a gnarled old aint that smelled of pine cones and mildew.

'Hold them still,' Pesticide hissed, pulling off her mittens to reveal her chemical blue fingers.

Behind her, the other flower fairies pulled off their mittens. Thistle's needle-sharp prickles bristled, Briar-Rose's long curved thorns glinted, and the tips of Nettle's black-nailed fingers glistened with venom.

'You *will* do as we say!' Pesticide insisted.

The four of them advanced towards Lord Asbow and the professors, their hands raised.

'Wait!' Mr Fluffy's voice rang out. 'There's a better way to get them to do what you want.'

Pesticide paused and stared at the

strange bespectacled figure in the tweed jacket who was in the clutches of a sycamore aint.

'Silence!' thundered Bert Shiverwithers.

'Wait,' said Pesticide, intrigued. 'Let him speak.'

'Take away their pets and lock them up,' Mr Fluffy blurted out, 'and the professors will do anything you say.'

'Fluffy! How could you!' exclaimed Lord Asbow, noticing the former experimental woodworking professor for the first time. He struggled in Bert Shiverwithers's woody grip. 'You traitor!'

'Release him,' Pesticide said. She smiled at Mr Fluffy and pointed towards the tree. 'I can be generous to those who help me,' she said. 'Take a gold muckle.'

Mr Fluffy bent down and plucked a gold coin from the heap of muckles beneath the tree.

'How could you stoop so low?' said Lord Asbow in a shocked-sounding voice.

Pesticide turned towards him, a

wicked twinkle in her eyes. 'Now take away the pets,' she told the aints, 'and lock them up in the farthest tower.'

The courtyard filled abruptly with barking, hissing, croaking, quacking, squawking and splashing as the aints separated the pets from their owners. While half the aints held the distraught professors in their grip, the other half carried off the dogs, cats, toads, ducks, parrots and the small goldfish in a glass bowl.

'Daemian! Daemian! Daemian!' the professors chorused tearfully as they watched their pets disappear.

'Now,' said Pesticide, turning to Lord Asbow, 'are you prepared to do what I say?'

'Yes. Yes, I am,' whimpered Lord Asbow.

Above them, the three moons of Muddle Earth rose majestically in the evening sky and shone down upon the courtyard . . .

'I want those instructions and I want them now!' demanded Pesticide. 'You will show me how to operate Whatever Castle, how to make it walk, run, stomp on things that get in my way . . .' She frowned. 'What's wrong? Why are you looking at me like that?'

In Bert Shiverwithers's woody grip, Lord Asbow struggled and squirmed. Thick black fur was sprouting from his face and neck as his body expanded. His nose turned black and shiny and elongated into a snarling snout. His hands and feet curled into claws and a thick stubby tail sprouted from the seat of his trousers. As the purple, yellow and green moonlight bathed the courtyard, Lord Asbow raised his immense canine head to the sky and howled at the triple moons.

Moments later, the most appalling smell rose up from his monstrously bloated doggy body.

'Pfwooaarrh!' exclaimed Bert Shiverwithers, dropping the gigantic werelabrador and staggering back, his twiggy fingers clamped to his knotty nose.

Around him, in the moonlight, the other professors were undergoing transformations of their own. A corpulent ginger werecat spat and clawed at Lichen Larry, while a huge warty brown weretoad sprang out of Mistletoe Mary's horrified grasp.

The rest of the Giggle Glade Mob struggled with deranged weregerbils, pink-eyed weremice and enraged wereguinea pigs. Meanwhile the Babbling Brook Boys weren't faring much

194

better, stumbling back under the attacks of squawking wereparrots and enormous quacking wereducks. Behind them, panic gripped the Dingly Dell Gang as a giant weretortoise with *Daemian* painted on its shell ran amok, barging the aints aside and snapping at their branches. In the middle of the courtyard, crammed into its bowl, an immense weregoldfish observed the unfolding chaos, one monstrous eye pressed up against the glass.

Pesticide and the other flower fairies huddled together beneath the muckle tree, their faces white with shock.

'What's happening?' whimpered Nettle.

'I'm frightened,' moaned Thistle.

'That goldfish, it's staring at me,' cried Briar-Rose.

195

'Bert Shiverwithers!' screamed Pesticide. 'Do something!'

Joe, Ella and Edward were dropped on to the cobblestones as the aint that had been holding them retreated with the others across the courtyard towards the gates. Joe felt a tap on his shoulder and looked up to see Mr Fluffy beaming down at him.

'You knew this would happen, didn't you, Mr Fluffy?' said Joe with a smile.

Mr Fluffy winked. 'It's a terrible thing for a wereperson to be separated from his pet, isn't it, Daemian?' he said, stroking the golden hamster that was peering out of the top pocket of his tweed jacket. 'Especially on a triple full moon.'

'He-e-e-elp!'

Joe turned to see the aints who had taken the pets come hurtling out of an arched doorway and back into the courtyard.

'We found the furthest tower,' babbled Mad Marion of the Wild Wood Crew, 'but when we opened the door, it was horrible!'

The aints of the Wild Wood Crew

196

swept past and headed after the others, who were getting into a tangle of roots and branches as they scrambled through the open gates. Echoing down the corridors of Whatever Castle came a cacophony of honking, banging and crashing, together with a monotonous chant of 'Cake! Cake! Cake!'

'Tower 101,' said Mr Fluffy ominously. 'It's where the poltergeese and the zumbies live. Not to mention . . .'

At that moment, through the arched doorway a strange phantom-like goose emerged into the courtyard, honking for all it was worth as it waddled on ghostly webbed feet. It was followed by a gaggle of others, clashing saucepan lids together and beating pots and pans with wooden spoons. Behind them, blinking into the bright moonlight, lurched a crowd of zumbies, portly undead cake-eaters, arms outstretched before them. Ancient crumbs encrusted their mouths and vintage jam stains streaked their woolly jumpers.

At the gates, the aints let out creaking cries of dismay.

THUD! THUD! THUD!

Following the poltergeese and zumbies into the courtyard came a black rabbit of frightening proportions. It stood on the cobblestones, its paws clenched and furry face scowling as its bloodshot eyes surveyed the scene. Then taking three massive hops it bounded up to Bert Shiverwithers and nibbled on one of his branch-like fingers.

'Ouch!' he shrieked, shaking off Binky the Black Bunny. 'That's it! I'm not staying here to become rabbit food!' He shoved his companions out through the gates. 'Aints!' he roared. 'Back to Elfwood!'

With that, the Babbling Brook Boys, the Dingly Dell Gang, the Wild Wood Crew and the Giggle Glade Mob

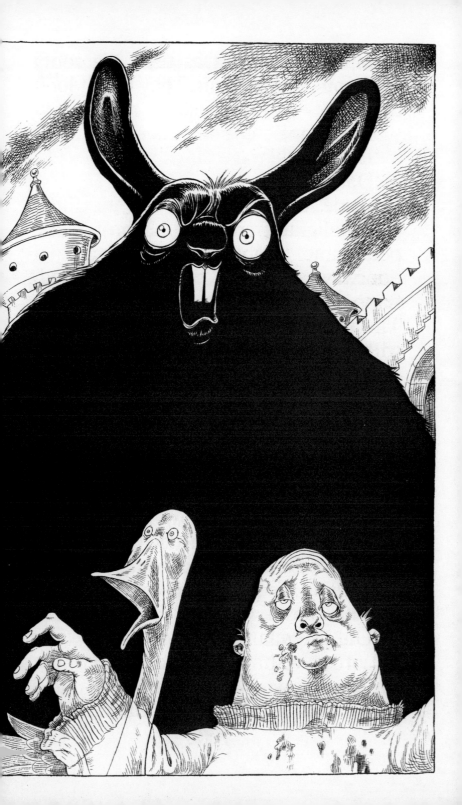

clumped off as fast as their big rooty feet would carry them. They didn't look back.

'Daemian!'

'Daemian!'

'Daemian!'

Inside the courtyard, the air filled with delighted cries as the professors' pets came tumbling from the arched doorway and ran, hopped, waddled, flapped and slid up to their owners. The instant Lord Asbow was reunited with his fat Labrador, he turned back to his former self, his claws retracting, fur disappearing and tail shrinking to nothing. In the middle of the courtyard, the pet goldfish in its bowl came sliding to a halt. The giant weregoldfish, its monstrous eye pressed against the glass of its own fishbowl, stared down at it. Moments later a decidedly damp Professor Quedgely picked up the bowl containing his pet goldfish and hugged it to his chest.

'Oh, Daemian,' he crooned.

Lord Asbow turned to the professors, who had all now resumed their human form. 'Munderfield.

Round up the poltergeese, if you'd be so kind,' he instructed. 'Stibbing. Chate. Take care of the zumbies. They've had far too much excitement for one night, poor things. There's chocolate cake in the pantry. Give each of them a slice.' Lord Asbow turned to the enormous black rabbit. 'Now, Binky,' he said gently. 'Hop along back to your tower, there's a good bunny, and Professor Quedgely will find you a nice juicy lettuce leaf, won't you, Quedgely?'

Professor Quedgely nodded and, tucking his goldfish bowl under his arm, led the black bunny away. Lord Asbow looked at the flower fairies cowering beneath the muckle tree, at the gold coins strewn across the cobblestones, and at the wreckage of the drawbridge at the castle gate. He shook his head and turned to Joe.

'This is why we don't encourage visitors, Jefferson,' he said. 'They do so upset everyone. Werepeople, zumbies, poltergeese—*all* our residents. Poor Binky is going to be having nightmares for weeks . . .' He sighed. 'You see, Jefferson, when you've lived here as long as I have, you'll understand that Whatever Castle is a haven for those who find it difficult to fit in here in Muddle Earth . . .' His gaze returned to Pesticide and her friends, who were pulling on their mittens and looking shamefaced. 'As you obviously do, my dear young fairies,' he said meaningfully.

'Lord Asbow!' came a brisk businesslike voice. 'I found these three fast asleep at the top of a tower.' An elegant woman with blue eyes, blonde hair and a dozy-looking wombat under one arm came striding across the courtyard, with Randalf, Norbert and Eudora Pinkwhistle in tow. 'I revived them with cups of my sunrise tea.'

'Well done, Mrs Couldn't-Possibly,' said Lord Asbow, and sighed. 'This has certainly been quite a day for visitors!'

'Fatso!' came a joyful squawk, and Veronica burst from Joe's robes and flapped over to Randalf.

'Veronica!' said Randalf. 'I can't tell you how glad I am that you're safe. I've been so worried . . .'

'Have you? Have you really, Randalf?' Veronica cooed, landing on the wizard's shoulder and nuzzling against his ear.

A shrill fanfare of bluebell trumpets sounded in the night air and a magnificent sleigh of woven meadow flowers on a blackberry-bramble frame came gliding through the gates of Whatever Castle. It was drawn by a dozen giant dragonflies ridden by fairy attendants in petal robes and followed by two grasshoppers in matching barley-straw top hats, their bluebell trumpets now tucked neatly under their arms as they hopped. The sleigh came to a halt in front of the muckle tree and its occupants climbed out.

'King Oberon and Queen Titania of

Harmless Hill,' one of the grasshoppers announced.

'Dad! Mum!' Pesticide exclaimed guiltily. 'It's not what it looks like— honestly!' She buried her head in her mittened hands and started to cry.

'It's precisely what it looks like, young lady,' said Queen Titania sternly. 'Can you imagine how I felt when I saw what you were up to in my magical viewing pool? Of course, we came at once to put a stop to it. Your father and I are very disappointed with you. With *all* of you. Aren't we, Ron?'

'Yes, Tania, my love,' King Oberon said, scratching his wobbly belly through his stained vest and looking unhappy.

Beside him, his queen drew herself up to her full height in her exquisite gown of camellia petals, stitched together with spider-silk and studded with rosehips.

'A muckle tree! I mean, really, Pesticide! Untold riches! An endless supply of gold coins . . . How vulgar!' Queen Titania sighed. 'Isn't that right, Ron?'

'Yes, Tania, my love,' said King Oberon, fiddling with his wand.

'I mean, that's not the way we brought you up,' Queen Titania continued. 'We got rid of all that old old fairy magic at the jumble sale before you were born, and buried all that vulgar gold. After all, who needs it with the wealth of nature that we have at our fingertips?'

'That's just it!' wailed Pesticide, pulling off her mittens and waving her chemical-blue fingers at her parents. She put her mittens back on. 'What chance have I ever had to enjoy the wealth of nature when everything I touch withers and dies?'

'And everything *I* touch gets stung,' said Nettle.

'And scratched,' said Briar-Rose.

'And prickled,' said Thistle. 'Oh, all I've ever wanted is a sweet little baby stiltmouse to call my own, to pet and stroke . . .'

Beside Randalf and Norbert, Eudora Pinkwhistle gave a stifled sob. Queen Titania spun round.

'Eudora?' she said quietly. 'Eudora the wicked fairy godmother. Is that you?' Her voice grew louder and harsher. 'I might have known you'd be mixed up in this somehow. Wasn't it bad enough that you blighted these poor innocent fairies' lives, just because your invitation to their christening got lost in the elf-post?'

'I've never liked the elf-post,' said Eudora quietly. 'That's why I invented the inter-elf—'

Queen Titania ignored her. 'An innocent mishap, but you wouldn't listen to reason. All the other fairy godmothers were so kind with their gifts of beauty, sweet temper and grace. But not you. Oh, no. You had to fly into a rage and put that horrid curse on my daughter and her three handmaids. What was it again? *With your fingers, nimble and spry, everything you touch shall sicken and die. As for your handmaids, one two three, their touch shall hurt all those they see!* You remember, don't you, Ron?' she said, her voice breaking with emotion.

'Yes, Tania, my love,' King Oberon replied, nodding sadly.

'Oh, I'm so ashamed,' Eudora Pinkwhistle wailed, falling to her knees and clasping her hands before her. 'Forgive me! Until this moment, I hadn't realized how effective my curse had been. But you must understand, I was young. I was impetuous. And I had the most awful temper. But I'm so much better now,' she said, wiping her eyes and scrambling to her feet. She reached into her black leather satchel. 'Please, let me put it all right . . .' She pulled out her magic wand and waved it in the air. *'Before these fairies go from bad to worse, may this wand remove my curse!'*

The four flower fairies looked at one

another as Eudora Pinkwhistle stepped back. Gingerly, first Nettle, then Thistle and then Briar-Rose pulled off their mittens and looked at their hands. The stings, the prickles, the thorns had all gone. Pesticide went last. She pulled off her black mittens and wiggled her fingers. They were now a delicate shade of pink.

'Oh, darling!' cried Queen Titania. 'Come and give Mummy a great big hug! You too, girls!' She opened her arms wide and Pesticide and the flower fairies rushed into them.

'I'm sorry, Mummy,' said Pesticide. 'We all are.'

'There, there, dear,' said Queen Titania. 'We can make a fresh start,' she added as she swept the four of them up in her arms and climbed into her fairy sleigh. 'Ron!' she called back. 'See to that dreadful tree!'

'Yes, Tania, my love,' said King Oberon, reaching out and touching the silver and gold muckle tree with the tip of his magic wand before jumping into the sleigh next to his wife.

As the dragonflies whisked the sleigh away Queen Titania shot Eudora Pinkwhistle a withering look. 'If I never see you again,' she called over her shoulder, 'it'll be too soon!'

The fairy sleigh disappeared through the castle gates and for a moment there was silence in the courtyard before, with a tinkling sigh, the muckle tree withered away, branches, trunk, roots, coins and all. Randalf rushed forward, Norbert at his shoulder, and stooping down, seized the battered old drinking vessel standing on the cobblestones.

'The Goblet of Porridge!' he proclaimed. 'I've got it! At last! My quest is at an end!'

Joe smiled sadly. 'I'm pleased for you, Randalf. Of course I am—but we're still stuck here in Muddle Earth.'

Beside him Ella and Edward exchanged miserable glances.

'And we're still no nearer to finding that lamp-post,' Joe went on.

'Don't worry,' said Randalf, patting Joe on the shoulder. 'Something'll turn up. It generally does.' He smiled. 'Trust me, I'm a wizard.'

'That's what you always say,' said Veronica.

'Shut up, Veronica,' said Randalf affectionately, tickling her tummy.

'Coo-ee! Coo-ee! Up here!'

Everyone looked up. There, flapping over the battlements and coming in to land unsteadily on the cobblestones, was Eraguff the eager-to-please dragon. His grey scales glinted in the moonlight as he folded his drab beige wings. In his claws he clutched a plump duvet. Unfurling it with a flourish, the dragon revealed the lamp-post, its legs tied up with three knotted pillowcases and a fourth pillowcase pulled down over its hexagonal glass lantern.

'You see,' said Randalf. 'I told you something would turn up.'

'It tried to get away but I was too quick for it!' Eraguff exclaimed proudly, pulling the pillowcase off the top of the lamp-post to reveal its glowing lantern. Just beside it, in the circle of yellow lamplight, the air shimmered and rippled like a puddle in the rain. 'I hope you're pleased,' the dragon said eagerly, smoke rings rising from his nostrils and floating up into the night air.

'Oh, yes, Eraguff!' Joe said. 'Very, very pleased! Aren't we, Ella? Aren't we, Edward?'

They both nodded, their eyes bright with excitement.

Joe rushed up and, wrapping his arms around Eraguff's scaly neck, gave him a great big hug. The dragon purred with pleasure. 'I'm just happy that I was able to help,' he said.

'The portal!' Ella pointed to the rippling pool of light. 'It's right there. That means we can go home.'

Joe turned to Randalf. 'It *will* take us home, won't it?' he asked uncertainly. 'We don't want to end up somewhere else—somewhere even stranger than Muddle Earth . . .'

'Oh, I think so, Joe,' said Randalf reassuringly. 'You see, worlds are like dandruff, remember? When you live in them for a while, bits of them stick to you. Bits of Muddle Earth brought you back here when you fell through the portal, and bits of your own world— from your own time and place—will pull you back when you step through the portal from this side.' He stroked his beard. 'Does that make sense?'

'N . . . Not really,' said Joe, and smiled. 'But I trust you. You're a wizard!' He hugged Randalf. 'I'll miss you,' he said. 'And you, Veronica,' he added, stroking the budgie's head.

'Good luck, Joe,' she chirruped.

'And me?' said Norbert, his three eyes blinking back his tears. 'Will you miss me?'

'Of course I will, Norbert,' said Joe, throwing his arms around the ogre. '*And* your prize-winning snugglemuffins!'

'Come on, Joe,' said Ella, who was holding Edward's hand. 'Before the lamp-post gets away again!'

Joe shrugged and he waved goodbye to everyone. 'Big sisters!' he laughed.

The air closed in around him as he stepped into the portal after Ella and Edward. Behind him, he was aware of the yellow glow from the lamp-post growing fainter. Soft fur coats brushed his face. They smelt of old ladies and banana skins. He pushed past them.

213

The next moment he tumbled out of the wardrobe and found himself in his big sister's bedroom, sprawling on top of Ella and Edward.

There was a creak and a groan, and the three of them looked up to see the flat-pack wardrobe disassembling and packing itself away. Planks, doors, screws, hinges, dowelling rods, door handles and instruction leaflet all neatly arranged themselves back in the cardboard box, which flipped itself over and disappeared into the rippling air.

A distant cry of surprise echoed between the worlds. It was Mr Fluffy's voice.

'The *Tumnus*!' it was saying. 'It's back!'

'Hello, clouds! Hello, mountains!' trilled a magnificent young dragon with wings of iridescent lapis lazuli, scales of opalescent cinnabar and underbelly of sparkling sapphire. 'Hello, everybody!'

Eraguff, the most eye-catching dragon in the Here-Be-Dragons Mountains, landed gracefully beside the mountain lake. The other young dragons, who had been waiting patiently to catch a glimpse of him, broke into rapturous applause.

'Isn't he marvellous!'

'Yes, so handsome . . .'

'And so nice with it. Not at all vain.'

'Apparently, a witch waved a magic wand over him and he hasn't been the same since.'

Eraguff stretched his long sinuous neck and sent a magnificent set of intertwining smoke rings coiling up into the air. The young dragons trilled their approval.

'As I always say, it's important to try to please,' Eraguff was pronouncing. 'Why, the best thing I ever did was give Miss Eudora Pinkwhistle a lift back to Giggle Glade when she lost her broom . . .'

With a sigh of satisfaction, headmaster Randalfus Rumblebore sat back in his big swivel-chair and eyed the Goblet of Porridge in the trophy case opposite. The honour of Stinkyhogs School of Wizardry had been restored, and he had Roger the Wrinkled's personally

216

signed letter in his pocket to prove it.

A few gold muckles from the High Wizard and Ruler of Muddle Earth in appreciation for all his hard work would have been nice too, thought Randalf, but still, one couldn't have everything.

In the corner of the study, Norbert the Not-Very-Big was sitting cross-legged on the floor, his findy bag in his lap. He sighed heavily.

'I had so many marvellous things,' he grumbled, 'until I lost them all, falling off that silly carpet. Now I've only got these,' he said to himself, 'an old trowel and this acorn thingy.'

He placed the two objects on the floor in front of him. At the desk, Randalf clutched the arms of his big swivel-chair.

'Trowel? Acorn?' he said. He scrambled to his feet and seized the Goblet of Porridge from the trophy case. 'Norbert, if I might have a little word . . .'

Crash! Bang! Wallop! Squelch!

'Peter, I can smell boiled cabbage and floor polish. And is that the nine-times table I can hear?'

'Oh, Susan, we're back. And look at the clock on the cloakroom wall. Only five minutes has passed. That means we haven't dodged detention after all . . .'

'But Peter! That's why we climbed into that howwible bwoom cupboard in the first place! What is that awful smell . . . Oh, Edmund, you haven't, have you?'

The stair-carpet sighed with contentment.

'I'm so in love,' she whispered.

Dyson the broom continued sweeping her intricate border of interwoven leaves, fruits and flowers.

From the far end of the corridor, Lord Asbow approached. He stopped at the foot of the impressive marble staircase of Whatever Castle's central tower. Dyson the broom stopped brushing and flew down to meet him.

Sweeping Lord Asbow off his feet, Dyson carried him swiftly to the top of the stairs and deposited him on the marble landing. The broom gave a little bow and returned to his brushing.

'I'm so in love,' the stair-carpet whispered again.

'Who'd have thought it?' said Joe to himself, and turned from the window as the roar of Edward Gorgeous's motorbike died away.

The former thumbsucking vampire from Muddle Earth had taken to his new life as if he'd been born to it, finding a job and a flat and even buying a Harley-Davidson to go with his fashionable motorcycle jacket. Mind you, he could afford it with the money he earned as the hottest new actor on the scene. If Ella was to be believed, her boyfriend had just landed the lead role in the new movie *Moonlight*—something about a girl falling in love with a vampire.

It sounded absolutely ludicrous, thought Joe with a smile. Still, he had to admit, everything had turned out rather well in the end. Both in this world . . . and in Muddle Earth too!